Edge of Reality

short stories

Mike Trial

Published by Compass Flower Press
an imprint of AKA-Publishing
Columbia. Missouri
www.AKA-Publishing.com

Edge of Reality

short stories

Mike Trial

Contents

Introduction

The reality we live in can sometimes shimmer into an entirely unexpected form. The eight stories in this volume illuminate the lives of people who have suddenly and irrevocably passed beyond the edge of their reality. And find there is no way back.

Grimoire

Black magic still exists, but today it resides in massive databases behind walls of security. And for the sorcerers who can read that electronic grimoire there is power enough to impose a new reality on all of mankind.

"Meet me. Today," Allen said. He seemed to be trying to whisper into the phone.

"I can't just drop what I'm…" I bristled.

He cut me off. "This is extremely urgent. Can you meet me in an hour?"

"Where?" I said, irritation clear in my tone.

"Don't say anything except yes or no to my questions; phone conversations are monitored. Remember last spring just after we graduated, we were driving around and stopped for a few minutes at a certain place. There was a full moon rising."

The image of the abandoned farmhouse came back to me. "Yes."

"Meet me there in two hours."

I glanced at my watch. Almost one o'clock. If I told my supervisor I needed to take the afternoon off, I could drive down to the abandoned house, meet Allen, and still be back in Omaha in time for dinner.

"Alright."

"When you get there, park under the trees," Allen said and hung up.

"Jesus!" I clicked my phone off. *Haven't heard from him in a year and now he needs to see me immediately. His phone is monitored. Park under the trees so your car won't be seen by spies in the sky? Is this guy paranoid or what?*

I considered ignoring him, but I couldn't quite ignore the desperation in his voice. I got in my car and drove down to Lincoln.

Route 97 looked exactly the same as it had last spring: an empty asphalt ribbon stretched endlessly between bare fields prepared for spring planting.

We'd found the old house by chance, Allen and me, one rainy Sunday afternoon when we were driving around with nothing to do. We'd both just graduated from the University of Nebraska— Allen in mathematics, me in engineering. And we both had accepted job offers—Allen with a firm called Datagenics, and me with Lockheed. Allen had already been at work for a week. My new job started Monday, so we'd told each other we'd get together, drink some beer, and reminisce about undergraduate days before we went our separate ways. But instead we found ourselves bored, driving around looking for something to do. Allen had never been a very social person; I was probably his only real friend, and now he seemed even more remote.

"It's getting late," I told Allen. "Time to go home." The rain had stopped, the moon was full on the eastern horizon, and a spectacular sunset was spread across the western sky.

Allen suddenly craned around, peering out the back window of my car. "Go back. I think there's an old house down that gravel road."

We bounced down a rutted gravel driveway under a canopy of rain wet locust trees. There was an abandoned farmhouse and some sagging outbuildings. The house was one of those old two-story frame houses that used to be on every farm back when I was a kid. Back when there actually were family farms, not today's ten thousand-acre corporate farms.

In the moonlight, the house looked spooky. Even though most of the windows were intact, the roof was sagging and the front door stood ajar.

Allen grabbed a flashlight and went up the battered porch steps and in the front door.

"Looks like a cheap horror movie set," I called after him. "Watch out for axe murderers."

I followed him in. The moonlight made the bare living room look very melancholy, but the wallpaper was unblemished, and the big plate glass window with its little cut-glass transom were unbroken. *No kids nearby to throw rocks through the glass. In fact, nobody nearer than Lincoln, thirty miles away.*

I envisioned this house as it had been once. A hardworking farm family, a nice yard under the trees, some flowers. *Probably worked their whole lives here, raised kids, sent them away to college, and the kids graduated and found jobs in the city. Can't make a living on small acreage anymore. And besides, farming is way too much work.*

I touched the molding around the door to the kitchen, worn from many hands. Now the old folks are dead, their farmland sold to Con-Agra, and the house is abandoned.

I heard Allen clomping around upstairs, so I felt my way up the narrow stairs. From the master bedroom window you could see over the tops of the trees to the endless flat fields of Nebraska. Allen came in flashing his light around. "Lots of these abandoned farmhouses between here and Denver." He ran his hand down the dusty wallpaper, colorless in the moonlight. "Agriculture is about economics, and small farms are no longer part of the equation."

"Your firm putting them out of business?"

He shook his head. "Nobody is putting anyone out of business. It's just that economies of scale require more acreage, bigger machines, more genetically modified seed, better herbicides. That's what makes farming efficient. And all that agro-industry is interdependent. Back when this was a working farm, these people could be self-sufficient. That's why the house was built down in this arroyo. They could put a shallow well down to water—that's it over by the windmill." Allen pointed out the window. "The trees shelter the house from the worst of the winter blizzards and the summer heat." He switched off his flashlight and let the moonlight fill the room with its pale glow. "That weed patch over there was probably their garden. They grew all their own vegetables, canned them for the winter. Kept a cow and some chickens."

He gave me a dark look. "The data we work with at Datagenics has shown me just how dependent we all are on corporate agriculture. That may not be good."

"Why?" I asked. "Can't turn back the clock on progress."

"Actually, you can." He found a stub of chalk in his pocket and started writing on the wall. "If you don't care who suffers for it." He was writing a line of symbols across the wall.

"Hey, this is still someone's property. You shouldn't do that," I told him, but he kept writing.

"Some people may want to go back to a simpler way of life," I told him, "but I don't. I want to explore. I want to go into space, Allen—maybe to the moon." I stepped to the window to admire the moon riding high over the treetops. "That's why I took the job with Lockheed. I want to be part of it."

But Allen wasn't admiring the moonlight, or listening to me; he was admiring the four-foot long line of symbols he'd written on the wall.

"You explore space," he said. "I'm exploring genetics." He pointed at the line of code. "Genome manipulation is all about working with codes mathematical codes. And manipulating very large date sets and checking outcomes of changes made at a genome level."

He drew two vertical marks, separating six or seven of the symbols in the middle of the row. "Clip these out and substitute different ones and you can modify a living organism."

"For example?"

"Soybeans."

I'm afraid I laughed. "Soybeans. You're not going to win the Nobel Prize for making better soybeans."

"Maybe yes, maybe no." He scowled.

"Sorry, I didn't mean to imply it's not important…" I changed the subject, trying to appear interested. "Looks like a line of hieroglyphs from inside the great pyramid."

"The ancients would have thought so, and in a way they would have been right. This genetic code could be called an incantation. The Datagenics Company's highly secure database is the grimoire from which it's taken."

"Grimoire?" I asked.

"From the old French word for grammar, a book of instructions. Later it came to mean a book of magic spells."

"That's the super-secret stuff you're going to be doing at Datagenics?"

"I've already started. Did some actual hands-on work during their three day orientation right after they offered me the job." Allen stepped forward into the growing moonlight, folded his arms and stared at the symbols. "We're doing world-class work. Prize winning. No wonder security there is tighter than at a weapons design facility." The wire rims of his glasses glittered in the moonlight.

He tossed the chalk in a corner and tapped the wall. "This line of code is an analog, not the real thing. Monsanto owns the real thing. We do contract design work for them and for Syngenta and the other big firms. Soybean genome designs have been patented since 1994, and since then various designs have been endlessly changed, trying to make them more efficient." He hooked a thumb at the vast prairie that surrounded the abandoned farmstead.

"The natural genome doesn't even exist anymore. Soy, corn, wheat and rice—the staples—are all entirely engineered, all patented, all designed to produce uniform growth densities and growth rates, so the equipment can be designed for maximum efficiency. Fixed ripening rate so the produce reaches the retailer at its peak condition.

All those rows of sweet, seedless, blemish-free fruits and vegetables we've grown accustomed to."

"I like what we have today," I told him, "but it's late, lets go home."

"Well, some people don't like it." Allen said following me down the narrow stairs. "Some people would like very much to disrupt the system. Datagenics puts as much time and money into security and genome self-protection as they do into experimenting with better designs."

"The anti-GMO hotheads going to storm your fortress? Destroy your database?"

"No, something much simpler: induce a virus that kills the plant as it sprouts."

"And starve three hundred million Americans?" We got in my car and sped down Route 97 in the moonlight. The road was straight as an arrow. No traffic. "That sounds like a doomsday device from the cold war. Why would anyone want to do that?"

"To force people back to a simpler life," Allen said quietly. "That kind of fanaticism makes religious terrorism look tame. And they can do it. Just infiltrate some researchers into our labs…"

I let Allen off at his apartment. "Keep in touch," I told him. He nodded but I knew he wouldn't. "And don't let anyone devise that doomsday device." I laughed. But he'd already turned away.

—————

Today, after his phone call, as I drove down to Lincoln, I couldn't stop thinking about our conversation last spring. *But that conspiracy to destroy our food, that's crazy. Fantastic. A megalomaniac plan to kill almost everyone so the survivors are forced to live a simpler life?*

"But even if this craziness is true, the government will stop it and we can rebuild with different crops after..." But then I remembered Allen telling me the natural genomes no longer exist. There's no way back.

The turn off to the old house was not easy to see. I passed it, then turned around, came back, and bumped down the rutted gravel under the thin shade of locust trees. I parked my Toyota beside a black Mercedes 600. *Datagenics must be paying Allen pretty well. Better than Lockheed is paying me.* The abandoned farmhouse hadn't changed. I went up the sagging porch steps and into the house. There was the same dust and gloom, the same sense of lives lived, now forgotten.

I found Allen upstairs, staring out the window at a green and yellow John Deere behemoth tilling a field in the distance. His hieroglyph was still on the wall.

Allen's suit was a stylish maroon double-breasted. His hair was slicked back; his glasses frames were an up-to-the-minute style. He looked like one of those sullen Armani models you see in fashion magazines. There was a slim black valise in his hand.

I started to joke that his grimoire must be paying well, but my words died as he turned toward me. I have never seen a man's face so twisted with fear.

I extended my hand for a handshake, but he thrust the slim black briefcase into my hand and shook his head. "We have no time. I must get back before I'm missed."

He headed for the stair.

"Now, wait a minute, Allen! I need some explanation." He kept going and I followed him. "What is all this cloak and dagger crap anyway? What are you dragging me into?"

In the gloomy living room he stopped. "The situation is more dire than you can imagine. Almost incomprehensibly so."

"It's certainly incomprehensible," I told him.

"Take that laptop home, turn it on and follow the instructions on the screen. There is a minor surveillance eclipse tonight. It's taken me months to arrange this. But it's too dangerous for me to try to activate everything from my... location."

"What will this thing do?" I said, indicating the valise.

His clenched jaw muscles knotted. "Help me stop the greatest catastrophe that has ever happened to the human race."

"What the hell are you talking about?"

"I have to go," Allen said, and went out, got in his car, and wheeled it around and ran the passenger window down. "Tonight at eleven o'clock, have that laptop running. Its signals will link with my signals from another location, and if all goes as planned, I can stop the insertion of certain viral forms that are being put into the genome of seeds that will be planted this spring." He tilted his head toward the field where we'd seen the John Deere working. "This will happen worldwide. The food research system is highly integrated. Not just soy, but wheat, corn, and rice, too.

"If I'm not successful, things are going to get very bad for a long time. You need to find a place to hide. This old farmstead would be the right place. You've got a few weeks to fit it up as a survival hideout. Tell no one what you are doing or where this place is. You'll have to live here without electricity, without fuel. Learn how to live off prairie plants and animals. It will be your only chance if the food system breaks down." Allen gave me a look. "And I think the crazies have found out that I'm trying to stop them."

"You're talking about nutcases threatening to kill six billion people! Who are these maniacs?"

"Back-to-nature, religious, who knows. Some kind of fanatics that think present civilization is not worth keeping. They've infiltrated Datagenics and other firms. They not only want to force all of us back to 'simpler' times, they want to be in charge of what's left of the world. They will be the new Pharaohs."

"Even if they succeed," I said. "We'll rebuild afterward. The human race always does..."

"Not this time," Allen said. "We can never rebuild again."

"Yes we can," I argued. "The human race is tough. We always rebuild after every disaster..."

"Not this time. We've burned the oil that's easy to get to, and the surface coal. Without that energy we can't rebuild technological civilization. We've used up the surface iron that can be smelted with peat fires. Without those basic energy sources and materials we can never again make engines, make medicines, communications. All we would have is stone, bronze, copper, wood fire, animal, wind, and water power. That's all."

"And you think someone is planning to do this?"

"I know they are. They're inside our organization, and other similar organizations. It's a fanatical back-to-nature conspiracy that may just succeed. And very soon. This planting season, maybe a month from now." He pointed at the briefcase I held. "Help me stop them." Then he ran his window up and drove off.

I got in my car and sat there in the shade, trying to decide what to do.

———————

"Crazy as a loon," I heard myself say. *But what if he's not? What if this fanatical conspiracy of naturists does exist and does plan to destroy civilization to force people to live 'simpler' lives. Insane, but possible.*

I opened the valise. Inside was an ordinary looking laptop. I closed it back up, and on a whim went back inside the musty old house and back up the stairs to the bedroom. I wondered if I could fix this place up in a month. Live secretly out here without electricity or fossil fuel of any kind. Get the windmill-driven water well working. Learn to live on prairie plants and wild game. Cook and heat with that cast-iron woodstove? In case there really was a conspiracy and Allen could not stop it.

I got in my car and drove back to Omaha. By eleven o'clock I had the laptop Allen had given me up and running. The instructions were simple. Some installed software came to life. I watched the screen for a few minutes, but all I saw was lines of numbers. The numbers changed several times, then stopped changing.

I sat staring at the screen for a few more minutes, then wandered out to the living room and glanced at the TV. The local news was on. A twisted black Mercedes 600 was being winched out of a ditch.

Ten years later

I stood in the upstairs bedroom watching the white face of the moon, remembering how I used to dream of going into space.

Before civilization ended, we were close. I would probably have been into space by now if a small group of people hadn't decided to permanently put mankind back in the Bronze Age.

Now all that mankind had, and all that we dreamed of…is gone. Gone forever.

We've cut the bottom rungs out of the ladder of technology and they cannot be replaced. All because a few crazies decided to become Pharaohs over people living a simpler life.

I guess somewhere out there they are, maybe in the Nile Valley, or the Indus Valley, or the Yangtze, just like the Pharoahs of ten thousand years ago. But the rest of us…will never venture to other worlds, other star systems, to search for other intelligences. The human race will die alone on this planet…. just as I will die alone in this house.

I made my way out of the moonlight and into the darkness downstairs and lay down on my cot to sleep.

The Finishing Touch

Their friends thought of them as the most perfect couple in all of San Francisco. But that was not reality. Love has long ago deserted them, money problems have arisen, and each of them wants nothing more than to be free of the other.

Tyler sat entranced, Cosmo in hand, watching the lights of the cars flowing by on the Embarcadero ten floors below Quentin's Bistro. But it wasn't San Francisco traffic that had Tyler entranced; it was Kristie. Warm, beautiful Kristie. The new love of his life.

Her warm ways, her loving touch, her exquisite taste in clothes and jewelry, and the black Mercedes she drove. The pride he felt knowing all the men in the place were casting covetous glances her way. Tyler loved it all.

"We need $400,000," Kristie said softly. "To pay Dan. And we need it now." Tyler drifted back from dreamland to focus on her soft brown eyes.

"I know," he said.

"Dan's been doing us a big favor," she continued, as though explaining something to a child, "Doing the remodel on our house without any money down."

Tyler had wondered about that, but, no sense looking a gift horse in the mouth. Besides the remodel was almost done and by tomorrow he'd have the money to pay Dan.

She glanced around the crowded Bistro. "Dan's often in here—maybe we should talk to him."

Tyler noted how several men's eyes furtively glanced away from Kristie when he looked their way.

"Yeah, you're right," Tyler said.

Kristie caught the waiter's eye, which was not difficult since he had been staring at her all evening. "Two more Cosmos," she told him.

Tyler, an Irish whiskey drinker by choice, pushed his half-finished Cosmo aside. "I can tell Dan positively that he'll get his money tomorrow." He was surprised at the confidence in his own voice.

"Once we get moved in," Kristie prattled on, "I want to start entertaining more. A lot more. Our apartment was okay, but no room for more than two or three couples at a time. At the house we can do it right, forty people, using the patio, with the fire pit to keep it warm.

None of those noisy gas heaters."

The drinks arrived in frosted martini glasses six inches across. *More is better?* Tyler thought, *this must hold a pint and half,* but Kristie liked them. They toasted.

"Why don't I pick you up at your office tomorrow at five," Kristie told Tyler. "We can drive out to the house and see how it's coming along."

Tyler, nodded, "Sure." He took both her hands in his, and for once she didn't pull back. "The deal I'm working on should close tomorrow. We'll have the money, so bring a bottle of champagne. We'll celebrate."

"OK," Kristie said. "There's Dan now," she said, raising her hand.

Dan Bolenden, owner of Bolenden Construction, shoved his burly form through the crowd, shook Tyler's hand, and gave Kristie a hug. "The best looking couple in the place."

Kristie beamed.

"We were thinking about dropping by the house," Tyler said.

Dan nodded. "Sure, make it near quitting time. Five-thirty or six."

"Tomorrow?" Tyler asked, not noticing the glance Dan shot Kristie and her slight nod yes.

"Tomorrow it is, then," Dan said. "Meanwhile, I need

to talk to those two guys at the bar. Lining up my next job."

"Great guy," Tyler told Kristie as he watched Dan back-slapping at the bar.

"Yes, he is," Kristie said. She seemed suddenly distracted.

———

The next afternoon, Kristie's black Mercedes 650SL was parked in front of First Fidelity's building when Tyler came out carrying a stylish brown leather briefcase. He got in and she pulled into traffic on Geary.

"Jesus, these windows are tinted so dark the cops are going to pull you over for being a gangsta," Tyler said.

Kristie laughed. "Who's calling who a gangsta? You're the one pulling these scams." She threw a glance at the briefcase on his lap.

"First Fidelity will never notice I skimmed $400k off their fees. Cash. Foreigners always like dealing in cash, and that makes it easy." Tyler lifted the briefcase a little. "Besides, what's $400,000 out of the twenty million First Fidelity charged Pacific Development for doing the property settlement. Which took a total of about four days of my time." He laughed.

A few minutes later they turned into the driveway of their house. Dan's truck was parked at the curb.

The garage door opened smoothly, Kristie pulled her car in, and the door closed behind it.

As they were getting out of the car, there was a sharp report, like a .22 being fired upstairs in the house.

"What the hell...?" Tyler threw Kristie a worried look.

Kristie laughed. "Nail gun." Another report from upstairs—and another. "Dan was showing me how they work. They're powerful…." She stopped and hurried up the polished oak stairs. Tyler was so taken with the view of her legs, he forgot to ask her when she had seen Dan and why she'd be want to know about nail guns.

On the third floor, the sheetrock was only installed on one side of the wall dividing the bedroom from the short hallway. As Kristie and Tyler stepped into the room, a Mexican construction worker put his nail gun back in its case and stowed it in the guest bedroom across the hall.

They heard him clomp down the stairs and say something to Dan.

Tyler set his briefcase on the floor and stood at the floor-to-ceiling glass window with a view of Transamerica tower and the downtown skyline in the setting sun. Kristie put her arms around Tyler and gave him a hug. "It's beautiful," she said. "Dan's idea for putting a third floor on this house was inspired," Kristie said. "This view is worth three times the $400,000 we owe."

Tyler nodded at his briefcase. "Owed. Past tense."

"I worry about you getting in trouble with First Fidelity," Kristie said softly, her eyes full of concern.

Tyler, aglow with her attention, told her, "Nothing to worry about. In these development deals, especially with foreign money, the principals want everything kept quiet, and they want the deal done fast before the regulatory agencies change their minds. They don't check the numbers that closely, just the bottom line." Tyler kissed her. "Let's celebrate."

She pulled away. "I forgot to bring the champagne. Give me a minute. I'll go down to the car and get it."

After she left, Tyler made a circuit of the room, then leaned against the wall admiring the view.

Kristie descended the stairs, careful not to touch the walls or the handrail. In the garage, she got in her car, touched the remote control, and when the door opened, pulled onto Bradford Street and sped down the hill toward Cortland Avenue while the door rolled smoothly shut.

In the upstairs bedroom, Tyler waited, leaning against the unfinished bedroom wall, a very self-satisfied smile on his face. *I have everything I could ever want: Kristie, a great house, no more money worries.*

There was a sharp snap from the other side of the sheetrock wall. Tyler's expression relaxed, his eyelids drooped, and he slid down the wall and lay in a heap on the floor.

Behind the wall, Dan put the nail gun back where his man had left it, stepped into the room, and scooped up Tyler's slim body. The head wound where the finish nail had driven deep into Tyler's brain had left an almost invisible mark.

Dan carried the body downstairs and out the patio doors and deposited it in a four-foot deep hole the new patio concrete would cover. Dan went back inside, took the cash out of Tyler's briefcase, and tossed the empty case on top of the body in the hole. Then Dan climbed into the Bobcat skid loader and placed dirt over the body, filling the hole to the top and more. He tracked the Bobcat back and forth over the dirt to compress it level with the grade line, then got out and reset the patio formwork and rebar he'd moved aside to dig the hole.

The concrete pump truck was scheduled to arrive at seven the next morning to place the patio concrete.

In the red glow of sunset in the bedroom, Dan took some spackle and filled and smoothed the two tiny holes the finishing nail had made in the sheetrock. Then he locked the house up and drove home.

———————

More than ten couples were gathered around the fire pit, their faces cheery in the ruddy light. The San Francisco fog haloed the party lights strung on the tall fence around the back yard.

"Great housewarming party, Dan," Bill said, shaking Dan's hand.

"Great house!" somebody shouted from the back of the crowd. Glasses were raised in a toast.

"And don't you two look good together," Cynthia whispered to Kristie. "I thought it was going to be you and Tyler...." Cynthia gave Kristie a glance. "Sorry. I shouldn't have mentioned—"

"It's alright," Kristie reassured her. "I'll admit I was hurt when Tyler disappeared. But when I found out later he'd embezzled money, I realized I was better off without him. And besides, by then I'd met Dan." Kristie turned on her dazzling smile.

Chris and Dora wandered over. "When Tyler ran off," Kristie repeated for them, "it hurt. But now, I think maybe I should have seen it coming. He was living way beyond his means, skimming money off the deals he did for First Fidelity."

"No!" Dora said. "He seemed so... honest. You two looked perfect." She glanced at Dan on the other side of the patio and stopped.

"Well," Kristie said, accepting another Cosmo from a passing server, "He's probably forgotten all about me by now. Probably lying on the beach in Mazatlan enjoying his new-found wealth."

Dora reached out and touched Kristie's hand. "You poor thing."

"Oh well." Kristie sighed. "It's finished."

A Life In Pictures

In a dying town in the Midwest, the old movie theater is closing its doors for the last time. And so, for Rafe, who lived only for the movies, the end is near—unless he can devise a plan to prevent reality from intruding into his imaginary world.

It was almost dark by the time I reached my old hometown, New Madrid. It had been a four-hour drive from Columbia, and I was tired of driving, but instead of going directly to the Ritz Theater, where I was pretty sure I'd find Rafe, I drove to the house where he used to live.

The empty house was unlocked, all the furniture auctioned off back in April after Rafe's mother died. Rafe's father put the property up for sale and moved. The 'For Sale' sign in the front yard was sun-bleached. New Madrid had been dying for quite a while. Real estate was not selling.

In the gathering dusk, the shadows seemed to make the old furniture reappear. The big armchair by the window and the couch along the back wall were specters in the darkness. I went upstairs, remembering to step near the side of the landing to avoid the creaking board, just like Rafe and I had done a hundred times when we were high school kids sneaking in late.

We'd been close as brothers then. This house was once as familiar as my own home.

The bedroom that had been Rafe's was dark, but the cheap bookcase under the window was still there, empty now. That was where he kept his collection of paperback science fiction books and his stack of *Strange Stories* magazines we had both loved. I'd come over Sunday afternoons when we were both twelve years old and we'd just sit and read. I can remember the covers of those magazines to this day. The table where his little thirteen inch black and white TV used to sit was gone. And with it all those *Outer Limits*, *Twilight Zone*, *Alfred Hitchcock*, and *Secret Agent* shows we used to watch. And all those 1940s movies, *Torchy Blane, The Falcon, The Saint,* all the old B movies from the 40s that our parents used to watch at the Ritz theater when tickets had been twenty-five cents and popcorn only a dime.

We watched them late Friday nights on Channel 13 with the sound turned low.

Rafe once told me, "I become those characters on the screen, when I'm watching, late at night. I can enter that world." The powerful imaginations of twelve-year-olds—but I'd felt the same way.

I stood there one more moment, listening to rustling of sparrows in the eaves. There was a strange presence in that empty house. Not ghosts of the past, but ghosts of what might have been, if Rafe's mother had not died, if Rafe's father had not moved.

Rafe and I had both been imaginative, quiet, self-sufficient kids, with parents perceptive enough and considerate enough to give us both the love and the space we needed.

But with his mother's death, that cozy world had disappeared. His mother's cancer had been fast, a few weeks and she was gone. Rafe's father was so shocked and hurt, he couldn't stay in that house. He moved to Sikeston sixty miles away. Rafe was to stay in New Madrid to finish his last months of High School, then he was supposed to come up to Columbia, be roommates with me, work during the summer, and we'd start our Freshman year together in September.

But Rafe never appeared in Columbia. I didn't want to call his father and ask where he was, and risk possibly getting him into trouble, so I said nothing. By the end of August I'd still heard nothing. That was when I decided to drive down to New Madrid, find him, and find out what was going on.

When I found no evidence of him at the old house, I parked on the street behind the theater and went in the little service entrance, which was unlocked.

Inside the main hall it was dark, but flickering light came from the seating area and a sound track muttered. A movie was running even though the marquee was dark and the front entrance had no lights on.

I entered the theater through the fire escape doorway. There was Rafe, lying on one of the couches he'd moved in from the lobby, staring at the flickering black and white on the screen.

"Hey buddy," I said. We shook hands, still awkward doing it but trying to be adults.

He opened a can of Busch for me and took another one out of the cooler for himself.

"*The Big Sleep*, Bogart and Bacall," he explained, eyes on the screen.

"Owners don't mind if you keep the place locked and watch movies all by yourself?"

"Place has been closed for two months," Rafe said nonchalantly. "But utilities are on until the end of this month. So why not?"

"You live here?"

He grinned at me. "Yeah. I've become part of the movies, just like we used to talk about. Virgil doesn't know I live in here."

"Your father thinks you're up in Columbia with me, ready to start class to tomorrow morning."

"I'm not going to be starting class tomorrow," Rafe said matter-of-factly.

"You're going to hide in here until when?" My tone was derisive, even though I hadn't meant it to be.

"Not much longer. Virgil's talking about having the Theater torn down." Rafe didn't seem concerned as he sipped his beer. "Don't know why he'd spend money doing that. Nobody's going to build anything here. This town is dead."

"If we're not going to be roommates at the University, what will you do instead?"

He lolled on the couch. "I hear army privates get paid $400 a month."

I took a big slug of my beer and shook my head. I knew Rafe hated the war in Vietnam just as much as I did, though we were careful never to tell anyone in New

Madrid. In that old town, going into the army right after high school was still considered an honorable thing to do. Lots of American flags were still flown around town.

"Or maybe I'll just get in my car and hit the road. Lots of people our age doing that. Maybe I'll sneak across the border into Canada. Dodge the draft."

I was aghast. Dodging the draft was unheard of in Southern Missouri, even in 1969 at the height of the protests against the war. I could no more conceive of dodging the draft, than of, well…anything.

"Best thing about living here in the Ritz all summer is all the old films stacked upstairs in the projection booth. The distributor knew the Ritz was closing so decided to wait to pick everything up next month."

"So you sit there, by yourself, watching these movies over and over? "

"Yeah. Another beer for the next movie?"

"Just one more. I need to get back to Columbia tonight and it's a four-hour drive."

Rafe's voice drifted down from the little slot into the projection room. "I'm a god to these actors. I have the power to make these characters live their lives over and over, any time I want."

Then our imaginations pulled us into the movie, just like always.

He started Dick Powell in *Murder, My Sweet.* I must have dozed off.

He nodded at the screen. "I can make them live, but I can't change their lives, they have only that one life." His look was thoughtful. "But I kind of like that predictability. And I like Hollywood's artificial versions of life, so much clearer, more interesting, than life itself." I heard a longing in his voice that had not been there before his mother died.

"I'm one of those guys...there," he pointed at the screen where people wearing LA 1940s clothing were passing on the sidewalk outside the shop window behind Bogy. "I think I lived there in a previous life. I want to go back there."

We used to talk about other lives and all that stuff when we were kids, upstairs in his room reading science fiction magazines and watching *Outer Limits* on TV.

"Maybe you'd like it, maybe you wouldn't," I told him. "There's more to life than what's in the movies. I plan to experience it all."

"Maybe you will, maybe you won't," Rafe said. "Most people don't. Take my old girlfriend, Sandra. After Mom died, she broke off with me. Now she's married and living in Sikeston, soon she'll be raising kids. Her husband will work all his life at Gates Automotive. Her life is as predictable as that." He pointed at the screen.

I stared at the screen for a few minutes trying to think what to say —how to convince him to get out of this little dark theater, come up to Columbia, and get on with his life.

"After we graduate, let's go on a road trip, like we used to talk about. Just get in the car and go. Anywhere. California maybe.

"Yeah, we'll do that," he said, and we both knew we wouldn't.

I turned back to the movie and must have dozed, because when I woke, the film was over and Rafe was gone.

"Rafe?" My voice sounded strange in the empty theater.

I found my way up the narrow stair to the projection room. The projector sat there, still turned on, the great white light glowing inside. The film had run all the way to the end and the machine had put itself on idle.

I never could find the light switches, so I walked up and down the aisles in the soft grey glow of the screen, but Rafe was nowhere to be found.

I couldn't search for him all night—I had to get going. It was already nearly ten o'clock. I still had the long drive ahead, so I got in my car and started north on I-55.

Christmas break I drove back down to New Madrid to spend the holidays with my parents. And as I drove along Main Street it took me a minute to realize the Ritz Theater was gone—nothing there but a level rectangle of frozen red dirt. It seemed very small for all the magic it had held.

Nobody in town knew what had become of Rafe.

My sophomore year I heard through a mutual friend that Rafe was missing in action in Vietnam. But somebody else told me that he'd run away to Canada. I thought about calling his father, but I never did.

The years went by, I graduated, got a draft deferment for defense work and went to work for GM. I got married, moved to Detroit, then to Sacramento, as I worked my way up the management ranks of the company. I gave less and less thought to New Madrid and Rafe.

Then one evening I was doing some work on my laptop and had the TV going. It took me a while to realize the movie playing was *The Big Sleep* with Humphrey Bogart and Lauren Bacall. It was the scene where Bogie's in the shop talking to the salesgirl while keeping an eye on Geiger's store across the street. People pass by the store window.

And as I watch, I see a man, dressed in a double-breasted wool suit pause and turn his head to look directly at me.

It is Rafe! I recognize him, and, fantastic as it seems, I know he recognizes me. He smiles, but his eyes hold a question. Then he turns and continues on his way, and moves off camera.

It was Rafe. I'm sure of that. He looked happy. But that hint of a question in his eyes? What was that all about? I puzzled over that, then finished my work and went to bed.

Later that night, I woke out of a sound sleep and realized the question in Rafe's eyes had been directed at me. Was I satisfied with my life? Had I gone out and experienced the world like I said I was going to? Or had I become one of those people Rafe talked about whose days go by as predictably and unchanging as characters in a movie?

Stone Cold

Driving west, running away from the ghosts of the Vietnam war, Trey spends the night in a rundown Bed & Breakfast that seems to be inhabited only by a crippled girl who lives as much in dreams as reality.

Driving west, into a towering prairie thunderstorm, Trey told himself he'd stop at the next town, but before he knew it, it was bucketing rain. He put the wipers on high, found an off-ramp and took it. He crept down a two-lane blacktop looking for somewhere to pull over. Hail started clattering on the roof of his new Dodge. "Damn! It'll trash the paint and the sheet metal." A sign he couldn't read went by, then another sign that said Historic Route 66. A gravel driveway appeared between two stone pilasters, he turned in and found shelter between two rows of cedar trees.

At the end of the driveway was a three-story stone house. His headlights illuminated a weathered sign: *Red Rose Winery – Bed and Breakfast*. He pulled into the narrow carport and let the Hemi idle its contented-cat rumble for a moment before he shut it off and went inside.

The tiny bell on the top of the door made a barely audible clink as he closed it behind him. A real oil lamp on a doily on a walnut side table was the only light. The room was cluttered with tables and chairs. Barely room to walk between them. He threaded his way into a dining room equally cluttered and equally dim. The acidic, pleasantly musty scent of wine casks filled the air.

"Hello?" he called, but there was only the distant rush of rain. He threaded his way through a narrow path between antique tables, sofas, easy chairs, and divans, past a long oak table with a flame-scarred top, and into an ancient kitchen. Another oil lamp burned on the zinc-covered counter. Hardly believing what he saw, Trey took in the hand pump at the sink and the real icebox where melt-water trickled slowly into a rusty trough. Dozens of cases of wine were stacked along the wall. He extracted a bottle, found an opener and a glass, and helped himself.

Chambourcin, the label said. Back in the dining room, he tried a wall switch, but no lights came on. He slumped onto a dusty sofa and put his boots up on a worn footstool. "Anyone here?" he called, not expecting an answer.

It was comfortable in the dim light, in the clutter and dust, with the dry, clear flavor of the wine on his tongue, and the sound of rain all around. Halfway through a third glassful, it occurred to him that, for the first time since he had gotten his discharge from the army two months ago, his mind felt at ease. The flame of the lamp was hypnotic. Sleep overtook him.

———

"Cresa?" Trey said, coming awake to the sound of thunder too reminiscent of NVA artillery. The rain had stopped, the room was silent, and the oil lamp burned low.

He realized a girl with long blonde hair, wearing a dark paisley dress of sixties elegance, was sitting in the red plush armchair.

"I'm Deidre," she said, making her way to his sofa in a curious fashion, hauling herself along with her hands on tabletops and chair backs. When she got closer he saw her withered legs dragging.

"I helped myself to some wine," he said. "I'll pay."

"Don't need to," she said. "Pour me a glass." She slid him an old-style glass with thick bottom and fluted sides and he poured it full. "These glasses were my aunt's," she told him. "She inherited them from her mother."

"Where is your aunt now?"

"Dead. My uncle too, and my parents. All gone."

She reached over and, with an elegant gesture, scraped a match and lit three tall candles that stood in tarnished silver. She tossed the smoking match onto the tabletop and settled herself onto the sofa beside Trey. "I saw your car out in the porte cochère." She said.

"That's what they call it?"

"The car looks new. Looks like it's your one true love."

He shook his head 'no,' but grinned. "So what?"

"My uncle was in love, but with his wine, not cars. Not his wife." Deidre continued in a chatty tone, as though they'd known each other for years. Trey liked that. "He made all this wine himself, from grapes right here on the property. Then he became old, withered and died, like his vines out there," she nodded her head toward the back of the house. "He always said that after he was gone, we'd have his memories in these bottles, his memories of hot summers tending the vines, of crisp autumn days picking grapes." Deidre drank a gulp. "Of crushing it and fermenting it, and aging it and bottling it, all that stuff." She took another generous drink from her glass and held it out for a refill.

"So you live here alone now?" Trey said. "No..." He searched for the right word but could find none. "Friends? No relatives?"

"No friends."

"I don't have friends either," Trey said. He felt light headed, disoriented. "No family either."

Deidre turned dark topaz eyes on his. "No friends, no family," she said in the same cadence he'd used, mocking him.

"Don't make fun of me." His anger rose in his face.

She watched that change with interest. "Your anger drives people away. No one is interested in someone else's pain."

"What's wrong with your legs?" he asked bluntly.

"A car crash," she said matter-of-factly.

He nodded and heaved himself up. "Mind if I open another bottle of wine?"

"Go ahead," she told him. "Any of the boxes in the kitchen."

He filled their glasses.

"You only think of yourself," she scolded. "You blame your hurts on others, but it is only the fates."

"Bullshit!" he said. But he remembered when Cresa, his girlfriend from before Viet Nam, had found him. He'd gone away. He hated himself for hurting her, but he could not be with her any more.

He had quit his job at the gas station and sat in his rented Budget Inn room drinking Busch and staring at the TV. *Art Grindle Dodge—the cars you want,* which after a while sounded like the truth. A red Dodge Hemi, that's what he would buy. He'd always loved cars; now he could afford one. His mind settled a bit, started to gain traction for the first time since he'd gotten out of the army.

Trey got up and paced the narrow tracks between pieces of dusty furniture. "I'm on my way to LA to make music."

"I doubt it," Deidre said matter-of-factly. "Your mind is as twisted as my legs." The room seemed airless.

"I don't need your bullshit!" He stood there fighting the urge to leave, and wondered why he was fighting it. "I've written music," he told her. "Good stuff."

She ignored him, heaved herself to the kitchen, and returned pushing a long-spouted galvanized oil can along the tabletop. She refused his hand with a peremptory flip. "Coal oil," she said. "There's no electricity." She took the chimney off the lamp that had gone out and poured fuel into the reservoir. A goodly puddle dripped onto the tabletop, which was scorched in numerous places.

She scraped a match from a big box of Blue Diamond's, lit the wick, and set the chimney back in place. Then, instead of shaking out the match, she touched it to one of the drops of spilled oil, which flared yellow. She lit another dribble, which lit a third. "The world is in flames," she intoned. "It is time to die."

Trey slapped his hands down flat on the flames. "What the hell are you doing?"

She pivoted away, scrabbled her way to the kitchen and returned with another dusty wine bottle in the big center pocket of her dress. "Open this."

He did, and poured them some.

"My uncle was very proud of his Vidal Blanc," Deidre said after they'd tasted it. "Insisted it be served cool, but not cold."

Trey sat down with the glass of golden wine and put his feet up on the torn velvet of an armchair. "I'm going to write music that people will listen to all over the world." He drank to dull the familiar feeling of worry, of urgency, of fear. "I've got a bunch of songs written, melody and lyrics. Worked on them back in 'Nam. In LA I'll start trying to sell them."

"Hurrying down a straight line," Deidre said

sarcastically. "To make music the whole world will hear? The gods will punish that hubris." She reached over and poured both their glasses full again. "Hurry to the highway's end, where your life will begin." She sipped. "Your life's already half over."

She heaved herself to a threadbare love seat and stretched out, regally swathed in her paisley purple and red. She raised her right palm toward him, and touched forefinger to thumb, the sign of Isis and Osiris. "Isis saved Osiris, but there was a price."

He stared at her, his irritation becoming a gentle breaking feeling. Memory—of who he had once been. "I know the myth. I used to be quite a reader." His expression darkened. "I'm not that person any more."

"And I used to be a princess in Tyre," she told him. "I still am. I return there in dreams; I return here to dream. One dream is no more real than the other. All things exist and always will."

"No they don't." Trey slapped the torn fabric of the sofa, raising a dust cloud. "Only this exists. We live and die by chance—one life, one life only." The mortar rounds fell on his firebase every night for a week. It was random chance who'd be found dead in the morning after the night's firestorm. He fingered the frayed cuff of his Levis. "Clotho, Lachesis, Atropos. Spin the thread of life, measure, cut. No meaning to any of it. I am alive, that's all I know, dammit! Listen to me!"

Her attention was on a book she'd opened.

"Why should I? You're just complaining. Where did you say you were from?"

"I didn't. Uh...Gainesville. Florida." He knew he sounded like he was lying even though it was the truth. She said nothing, returned to her reading, but the candles had burned low, so she got more and lighted them. He liked seeing her face close to the flame, her eyes on the light, deep chiaroscuro.

"Flames. The world will end in flames just like these. Götterdämerung," she said, putting the matches down. "It's not random chance." She tossed him a look. "That's for people, stupid people." She came across to the deep red couch where he sat and looked him right in the eye. "People do stupid things. The gods laugh," she told him. "The world's in flames: Detroit, Berkeley, Watts, Paris."

The dusty scent of the highlands drifted across his memory, unwanted. Dust and diesel, helicopter turbines, distant scent of napalm, the shit-house at the concertina wire. Hazy, hot days and rotting nights, when the rats were wavering shadows between the hooches. Helicopters overhead in dim blackness, and once, when the nightly mortar fire had set off one of the ammo dumps at Khe Sanh twenty klicks away, the red glow—like the fires of hell.

"You think you will be the one to make a new Rome," Deidre taunted. "Sail your Dodge across the endless sea of grass. Make music to change the world." She shook her lank blond hair. "Music changes us, we don't change it."

Trey got another bottle of wine. "A Phoenician princess," he muttered, sarcasm in his slurred words. But the alcohol had eased doors open in his mind. Memories glowed, of a different person a different place, a different time. "I remember," he whispered sitting down heavily and taking a swig from the bottle. "Virgil's story."

"You can't change the world," Deidre said bitterly. "You can't change anything." She held her topaz gaze on the oil lamp. "Stone gods hold us all... frozen in time. Otherwise I would drift away with the night rain." Trey opened the draperies. The rain had stopped and the pleasant scent of wet cedar crept in.

"Why do you stay here?" He sat down beside her. "Get someone to take you away from this place."

"Why do you drive a highway that never ends?"

He put his face close to hers, to talk her out of all she was saying, but she put her lips on his, not quite a kiss.

As he leaned forward, she pulled away and rolled over and over on the sofa to the corner where a pile of worn paperbacks lay within reach. "My empire is here." She lolled her head this way and that. He came closer, but she said a silent no, so he backed away and found a corner where he could lean against cracking wallpaper.

"I'll be leaving soon." He craned to see his car in the dim light of the porte cochère.

"Your car. Freedom," she told him.

"I go where I want."

"Nowhere," she said. "Go fast, through all that emptiness, but when you stop nothing has changed." Her iridescent purple lip-gloss seemed to fluoresce in the yellow light.

Trey pushed off the wall, intent on leaving, but his body steered him to her. He lay on the couch, took her in his arms and she did not resist. Pressed close together, she did not seem disabled. Her body was warm. She continued to whisper as though he were not there, which was all right with him. For a while, he just wanted to hold her.

"The stone-gods deep in the black water of that old quarry hold people here. Keep them from achieving their dreams. There is an abandoned quarry near here..."

"I know," Trey said. "I almost drove off into it in the rain. That curve is sharp."

"That quarry has been abandoned for fifty years. Now there's water in it. Deep dark water—perfect still, absolutely black. Nothing lives in those waters. They are not farm ponds with bluegills or woodland streams with dragonflies and frogs and turtles. The quarries are haunted, by ..."

"By what?"

"Gods of stone," Deidre said.

His mind opened. He remembered the Trey who had been a naïve grad student in English literature, still filled with the glory of language even after four years of study and the draft hanging over his head. He learned he could live inside his mind. As he lived through the endless army days, he composed melodies and lyrics in his mind. He wrote his songs down in a tiny notebook and sometimes sat dreaming of his music being played, recorded, and transmitted over radios everywhere.

Trey said suddenly. "Dido of Carthage."

"Princess Dido, if you please," she corrected him. "My father was a king."

"Am I Aeneas?" he asked. "Destined to leave you behind? On my way to found the greatest empire the world has known?"

They both laughed, but they both wanted to will it into being.

"You died," Trey said.

"The doctors say I am suicidal," Deidre said to the collar of his tee shirt. "And delusional." She nodded at a cluster of orange plastic containers with white tops. "They tell me to take antidepressants. Sometimes I do. Want some?"

"The VA docs told me the same thing. I quit going to the VA hospital."

"I don't talk to the doctors any more," Deidre said. "I don't talk to anyone. No one comes here. I'm safe." She pushed herself close to him.

His mind trembled open again. He thought of the two of them, ordinary people, living ordinary lives in an ordinary LA suburb. It could be done. He felt warmth for her. *I could take care of her*, he thought. He sat very still, examining the thought.

She nestled at his side. He pulled himself slowly away from her and told her, "This is not what I want. This is a prison. I can't take you with me, because you would make anywhere I went a prison. The road. That's a gift from the gods. Go fast..."

"You bastard!" She hiked up her paisley dress to show him her twisted legs. "This is my gift from the gods. My husband was Christian, went to the church and prayed every week, but it did not save him. A brand new 1967

Ford Galaxy 500 XL with the 427 engine performance pack," she recited. "He had to have it. Just like you."

She glared at Trey. "Killed him, crippled me. I'll never walk again, and I'm supposed to welcome my gift from the gods?" She snapped her dress back down. "Drive to the ends of the earth for all I care. The stone god will find you and hold you paralyzed."

"Bullshit!" He reached out to touch her, to ameliorate her anger and her sorrow, and a moment later they were making love on the old couch under the threadbare blanket. Her withered body was not troublesome for Trey, but the darkness in his mind caused him trouble, and for a while it was awkward, but eventually, it became right.

He woke when she rose in the darkness, pulled on a robe and levered herself to a dressing table with a mirror. She lit a candle and looked at her face, one side, then the other. She took a pair of scissors and cut a small lock of her blonde hair and put it in a locket, then hobbled back to the sofa where they had made love, and pressed the locket into his hand.

"Keep this with you. When I die, it will save me." She closed her eyes and he pulled the blanket up over her twisted body. He luxuriated in having his mind free of darkness for a while.

But when he drifted back into sleep, a familiar dream recurred. Artillery fire, incoming whistling screams, one round the gods had designated for him. Whistling down at him in dead silence, then vanishing at the last minute. He woke, sweating, heart pounding.

Deidre slept, looking angelic. He touched her blonde hair, then rose silently and pulled back the velvet drapes. A thick pink fog lay over the driveway and the cedar trees. He pulled on his Levis and faded Gainesville Kustom Kar tee shirt and went out to his car. He felt her locket as he dug the car keys out of his pocket.

He knew she would wake when he started the car, but that couldn't be helped. He needed to get away. She was crazy and staying here in this dark stone prison would make him crazy. Taking her with him would be even worse.

He fired up the engine and started down the driveway in the thick fog. He turned onto the blacktop and caught a glimpse of a yellow glow in the rearview mirror. He couldn't take his eyes off it. "Crazy bitch," he said. "She's set fire to the house." He stared at that yellow light, for a second, then another second. He could go back, save her, take her with him. He shook his head and turned his attention back to the road ahead, but it was too late. He'd missed the curve veiled in the fog.

He slammed on the brakes, but the big Dodge was already sliding off the asphalt, through gravel, and through the painted wooden rail that marked the edge of the quarry.

In free-fall, the car tilted nose-down and fell a hundred feet to the black surface of the water, and in that instant of free-fall in blackness, Trey felt a wild elation, a freedom he had never felt before. The car impacted the dark water with a shock like the blast of the 152 mm NVA artillery round Trey had expected every hour of every one of his 365 days in Vietnam.

His life was erased in an instant.

The car sank slowly, still holding its perfectly vertical posture, gas and oil burbling up in iridescent psychedelic whorls in dawn's rosy light.

Eventually the Dodge's front grille touched the rocky bottom; it stood motionless. Trey's mangled body drifted down to lovingly embrace the steering wheel. He bore Deidre's locket with him down to the realm of darkness, never knowing how much it had eased her suffering.

———

The Dodge was never found, because no one ever looked for it. Of The Red Rose Winery there was only scorched stone.

"Must have been arson," the townspeople told each other. "Nobody's lived there since the old couple died."

The ruin of the house and the neglected vineyard are for sale, but there have been few inquiries, though now there's talk of a developer willing to bulldoze the property to make tract housing for fast growing Springfield. They say the cheapest way to get rid of the old stone will be to bulldoze it into the old quarry.

Shock Theater

In the 1950s many TV stations ran horror movies late at night on shows hosted by mysterious women named Elvira or Zelda. One memorable Friday night the viewers of KRCR's Shock Theater *got a glimpse of something much more horrifying than anything they could have imagined.*

A candle in a skull on a small table provided the only light. Dry ice fog drifted across the floor. The red eye of the TV camera glowed. Zelda, chained to a maroon velvet chair, stared into the darkness with terrified eyes. Her skin was pallid as death itself, her hair jet black.

There came the sound of an uneven tread, and a shadowy figure materialized and drew forward into the flickering light. It was Hugo, the zombie, his expression tortured.

"No! No...!" Zelda sobbed, but Hugo advanced on her, raising a knife in one hand.

The same old army bayonet I told him to get rid of, Zelda thought. *This is supposed to be a Transylvanian graveyard, not an army surplus store!*

Zelda rose, the chains slipping off her wrists. Her crimson red lips parted, revealing long vampire fangs. "My sorcery breaks these bonds!" she exulted. She stood, hissing, and raising a slender right arm, commanding obedience. She pointed a glued-on claw at Hugo, the zombie, who paused in mid-stride. His bayonet fell onto the studio floor and was lost in the fog.

Zelda turned to the small table with the glowing skull. There was the brief, muted sound of a cigarette lighter and Zelda picked up a long cigarette holder with a smoldering Kent in it. She waved the cigarette at Hugo, who cowered, nearly knocking over the plastic headstone on the fake grave.

"You are in my power," Zelda intoned. She turned to face the TV camera, her long black dress swirling. "*All* of you are in my power. And tonight I command you to watch *Invasion of the Body Snatchers,* starring Kevin McCarthy and Dana Wynter."

She had to hurry her lines before Hugo burst out with some unscripted diatribe like he had last week, and the week before.

"Set in a small California town," Zelda continued, "Dr. Miles Bennell finds people have been replaced by creatures from outer space."

Hugo lurched up, waving his retrieved bayonet, which had a wicked edge to it. "Yes, creatures like that!" Zelda improvised, shrinking away from him.

Hugo advanced on the camera, but fortuitously the red light blinked off and the movie began. Hugo stopped short and looked down at his bayonet. Then he slunk off down the hallway to his dressing room where she knew he kept a bottle of Jack Daniels. Zelda, in real life Alice Martin, was a part-time secretary, and "production assistant" at TV station KRCR. This entitled her to play Zelda the Vampiress host of *Shock Theater* every Friday night for an extra $100 a week. She had to pay for her own costumes and makeup.

Got through the first cut-in, Alice thought. KRCR's automatic equipment would run the movie until she pushed the button for their second skit at midnight.

She sat back down in her velvet chair, kicking a roll of duct tape into a corner. "This place," she muttered. "What a dump." She'd had to ask the day-shift guys to tape the leg back on the rickety table after Hugo had put his weight on it last week and broken it.

Their cut-ins would be better if she could rehearse more with Hugo. But that would mean spending more time with Hugo, and Alice was a little afraid of him. His costume was truly filthy, he smelled bad, and he had alcohol on his breath.

However, she did have some help rehearsing. For the last month she'd been dating Frank Ferguson, the young sportscaster at the station, who had been helping her write and practice her lines.

Popping out the plastic vampire teeth, she put the cigarette to her lips. She liked Frank, and she believed he felt the same about her. She hoped he did, anyway. She walked down the dark hallway of the deserted TV station to stand outside the front door.

Halloween night 1957 was cool and crisp; the stars sparkled, and the lights of Kirksville were clear in the distance.

A familiar white Lincoln Continental pulled into the parking lot and her boss, Bill Schaub, KRCR's station manager, got out. He was a big beefy man, flaunting a Burt Reynolds mustache and mutton chop sideburns. His belly threatened to explode the satin shirt he wore under a sky blue polyester leisure suit jacket.

"Hi Bill," said Alice. "What brings you out here this time of night?"

"You," Bill said shortly, "and Hugo, and the *Shock Theater* time slot. We need to talk."

Alice's heart sank as she followed him into his roomy office where he sat down at his desk and lit a cigar.

"Alice, I'll come straight to the point. I'm canceling *Shock Theater*, replacing it with drama and comedy movies, not fantasy. And I won't need you two as hosts for those movies."

"Jesus, Bill, that's sudden," Alice gasped. "I guess I can get by on my part-time secretarial—"

"Sorry, Alice, but I'm eliminating your part-time position, too. We've got to cut costs. Margaret can handle both the secretarial stuff and the FCC stuff."

He contemplated the ceiling. "Right now, *Shock Theater* has only got one sponsor, Marlon's Used Car City, which brings in $200 a week. And the only reason Marlon sponsors the show is so he can watch himself on TV while he's drinking beer with his buddies. Other local merchants aren't going to buy ads when the movies we show are these horror films. I want realism, drama, comedy, not crazies with rubber knives."

He handed her a white envelope. "Here's two weeks severance pay, plus your salary for this week. Tonight's show will be your last."

Alice went to her desk, fighting tears. *To hell with Bill Schaub*, she thought as she dumped her personal stuff into a cardboard box. As Alice carried the box out to her old VW Beetle, Bill leaned out the studio door and yelled over to her, "Hugo in his dressing room?"

She shrugged.

"Jeez! That guy is never around," Bill shouted. "I drive out here in the middle of the night to talk to him and I can't find him! Jeez!"

He paused, holding the glass door open. "Tell you what, you two don't even need to do your second skit tonight. You can leave right now. We'll show Marlon's advertisement then go straight back to the movie." He went into the building and disappeared down the darkened hallway.

Alice pulled a cigarette out, then pushed it back in the pack. *Well, I guess that's that.* She turned to go inside and get her costumes from her dressing room, but stopped. *Why am I taking my time to haul off a bunch of thrift store costumes? Let Bill Schaub throw them away.*

She got in her car and drove off, not really caring where she went as long as it was away from KRCR. As the cool night air flowed by, she found herself smiling. *I'll go by Frank's apartment, surprise him with my fright makeup. That's what I'll do.*

"Don't be too eager," she told the night wind. "Frank's a great guy, but he's leaving." Her smile faded. He'd just told her today when they'd had lunch together.

———————

It had been a gorgeous autumn day, sparkling blue sky, white clouds, bright sun and they'd decided to take their lunches and picnic at bench on the Missouri State campus. But it was clear Frank was not seeing the beauty of the day. Frank seemed unusually quiet, so she didn't bother him with questions.

When he finally spoke, it was almost like he was talking to himself. "I want to be something more than a part time sportscaster and host of a kids' dance show. KRCR is the only station in this town, and Ed Schaub has made it clear to me that what I've got now is all I'm going to get. He's trying to cut costs." Frank studied his hands. "I may get out of TV. Maybe go into advertising or something."

"Oh no!" she gasped. "You shouldn't do that. You're a natural in front of the camera."

He shook his head. "Maybe, but there's no opportunity for me to grow my skills at KRCR."

"Everybody loves your *Dance Party*," Alice said, trying not to sound desperate. "You do a great job."

"Yeah," he said, a little embarrassed. "I'm the Dick Clark of Kirksville. But I don't want to be doing *Dance Party* when I'm fifty years old." He brightened. "Last week I did phone interviews with a couple of Chicago companies' advertising firms. One of them made me an offer."

"I'm happy for you Frank," Alice said in a small voice. They finished their lunches in silence and returned to the station.

———————

Alice turned down the street to Frank's apartment.

Bill Schaub, you bastard, she thought. *You could give Frank a shot at doing the news, or hosting his own talk show. With all your cost cutting, I'll bet you didn't cut your own salary one bit.*

The street was deserted this late; the little trick or treaters already returned home to gorge themselves into a bellyache.

Alice parked her Volkswagen, checked her fright-makeup in the rear view mirror, then popped in her vampire teeth, quickly crossed the lawn, and rang his doorbell.

When Frank opened the door he nearly dropped his can of Stag. "Holy cow!" he gasped. Zelda the Vampiress showed her vampire teeth, claw nails poised to strike, face chalk white, eyeliner jet black.

Then she laughed and dropped her pose. "Going to invite me in?"

He grinned. "Sure."

His apartment was spartan. A vinyl and Formica dinette set, a couch, an armchair and a black and white thirteen-inch TV. It was tuned in to *Shock Theater*, Alice noticed.

"All I've got is beer," Frank said uncertainly.

"That'll be fine."

They settled onto the couch, close together but not quite touching.

"Don't you need to get back to the studio to do your second bit soon?" Frank asked.

Alice took a drink of her beer and told him about Bill Schaub firing her.

He put his arm around her. "I hate to hear that," he said. In a moment they were kissing.

When Alice pulled back, to cover her embarrassment at being so forward, she said, "Bill's out at the station now, firing Hugo. Bill told me I didn't need to come back and do our second segment tonight. So here I am."

"I'm glad," Frank said and kissed her again.

"It is Halloween, you know," Alice said with a coy smile. "Trick or treat?"

He laughed. "I'll take the treat." And they stayed in each other's arms for a while pretending to watch *Invasion of the Body Snatchers.*

"I was wondering," Frank said slowly. "I won't be leaving for a while. Since you're now unemployed, you could drive up to Chicago and we could check out the city together."

Alice felt her heart surge. *Go slow*, she told herself. "Let me think about it. I'd love to do that, but I've got to think about it, OK?"

Frank looked into her blue eyes. "Sure. You do need to think about it. I don't want you to feel like I'm rushing you into something." Then he smiled his infectious smile. "But it would be fun, you and me, exploring Chicago together."

"I know it would," she said. And she knew right then that she would meet Frank in Chicago.

"Speaking of Hugo," Frank said, "which we weren't. I ran across him today."

"Hugo? Really?" Alice's mind was still on Chicago.

"Yeah. I was on campus getting copies of my graduation certificate and there he was, sitting on one of the benches on the quad...."

"Watching the girls, of course," Alice said, her attention returning. "That dirty old man. He scares me."

Frank frowned. "Yeah, he's not quite right in the head. Apparently he was in combat in Korea and it messed up his head pretty bad. I really didn't want to hear it, but he kept on and on about the night attacks."

Frank finished his beer. "Hugo said 'When you hear them tank tracks clattering out in the night, you'd better run, run like you've never run before. We all ran like hell. Some of us made it.' He must have told me that three times."

"That's terrible," Alice said. "I feel sorry for him, but I still don't like being around him. In a way, I'm glad I'm leaving—have left—the station."

Frank, his eyes on the TV, continued, "I asked Hugo why he wanted to play the part of a zombie, and he told me 'Because that's who I really am. Doctors at the VA don't understand. Nobody understands.' "

"Poor guy," Alice said. "I'm pretty sure he's homeless. I think he keeps a sleeping bag stashed in his dressing room. Once Bill fires him, I don't know what's going to happen to him."

Frank glanced at his watch. "Isn't it about time you and Hugo would normally do your second cut-in?"

Alice lit a Kent before noticing there were no ashtrays. She quickly extinguished the cigarette in her empty beer can.

"Yeah," she said, trying to be nonchalant, but with a catch in her voice. She smiled wistfully. "We'll see Marlon's Used Car City ad, then back to the movie. I guess you could say *Shock Theater* has already disappeared…" Her voice trailed off as she stared at the TV. "What the hell?"

The picture on the TV was not Marlon grinning from his used car lot, it was the *Shock Theater* set. A man was duct taped to a chair.

Frank and Alice stared at the TV, speechless.

The man taped to the chair was big and beefy. He struggled against the unyielding tape. His mouth worked beneath the tape.

There came the shuffling sound of boots on the studio floor, and then Hugo stood over the man waving his army bayonet. With a glance at the TV camera, Hugo raised the bayonet and plunged it into the man's chest. Blood spurted.

"My God!" Alice gasped. The victim kicked and struggled. The chair toppled over, taking him out of range of the camera, but Frank and Alice could see Hugo's arm rise and fall, the knife blade dripping blood.

After a moment, Hugo rose to his feet, saluted the camera, and disappeared from view. The Marlon's Used Car City ad began.

"What the hell was that?" Frank said in a shaky voice.

They jumped in Frank's Mustang and drove out to the studio. When Frank turned the engine off, the night was dead silent.

"I'm scared," Alice said.

"Bill's Cadillac is still here," Frank whispered, opening the Mustang's door silently. They went inside and crept down the darkened hallway. All was silent except for the whisper of the movie from the monitor in the control room.

In the little *Shock Theater* studio at the end of the hall, they found a man on the floor, taped to a chair and covered with blood. A bayonet protruded from his chest.

Bill Schaub, star of his own short-lived—but very realistic—TV show, was dead.

Over the following weeks the police searched for Hugo, but he was never found.

Phone calls and letters to the station called that fateful night's *Shock Theater* the best they'd ever seen.

Dark Fire

In the year 1900, Robert Snyder used part of his fortune to build a private retreat in a remote part of the Ozarks. But the great stone walls of his mansion could not protect him from greed and lust and envy.

Robert Snyder laid aside his newspaper and shouted for the butler. "James! Build up the fire."

Outside on the mansion terrace, Sylvia and Kenyon cavorted, oblivious to the late October cold. Howard huddled out of the wind, his eyes always on Sylvia.

Sylvia was a fresh-faced Irish beauty, an employee of Snyder and Sons, who Robert Snyder had brought for a week's vacation at his mansion on a crag in the Ozarks along with his sons Kenyon and Howard. She was just the latest in a long line of young immigrant women who Robert used for a week or a month, then discarded.

Robert stood at the window watching her wave her

red silk scarf in the wind, trilling a laugh. Kenyon put his arm around her, but she danced away from him, while a wave of resentment surged through Robert. *Kenyon relishes pushing me, blast him! Flirting with Sylvia right under my nose.*

Fuming, Robert picked up the movie camera and wound up the clockwork drive. The camera, tripod, and the hulking film projector were gifts from none other than movie mogul D.W. Griffith himself.

The expensive gear had been delivered to Robert's office the previous week by Slidell & Son's Eyeglass and Mechanicals shop.

What the hell do I want with these contraptions? Robert had thought. But he wouldn't turn down a gift from a mentor. Griffith had helped Robert get started many years ago, and as Robert prospered, he had in turn invested in several of Griffith's films. *From which I've yet to see any financial return.*

"After you make a movie, the film has to be processed. We do that right here in Kansas City," the younger Slidell said proudly. "You're the owner of the first private movie projector in Kansas City. All the rest are in theaters." Slidell Sr. patted the giant projector fondly.

"Movies," Robert snapped, "are a waste of time." But he picked up the heavy camera and let the Slidell men show him and his two sons how it worked. *Best to pretend to be interested in the gift.* The men explained how the projector worked while Robert fidgeted, fingering the gleaming chrome gears. Operating machinery was servant's work; he didn't need this time-consuming explanation. After a while longer he dismissed the Slidells and his sons. "Fine. Kindly deliver it to my house."

Slidell junior nodded.

"No—" Robert amended. "Kenyon, Howard, show them downstairs and add it to the cart taking our luggage to my mansion in the Ozarks." Robert grinned. "Can't have it sent to my house here in town, you know. Wife wouldn't like it. Women are scared of machinery."

And you're scared of her, young Slidell thought. The Slidells knew, as everyone in Kansas City knew, that Robert and his wife Agnes remained married strictly for propriety's sake—they had detested each other for years.

"We'll have some film for you to process within a week," Kenyon blustered. "We're departing for the mansion today."

"A caution, Mr. Snyder," Young Slidell said as he laid the camera in its box. "The film is made of nitrocellulose, which is quite flammable…."

"Camera heats up?" Robert asked, seating himself behind his desk.

"No, the film projector does. It uses burning carbon rods to generate the necessary white light. But the film must roll past those rods quickly or it will overheat. Run it too slowly and there could be fire."

"Then I'll make sure I have a smart servant running it," Robert laughed. "If such a thing as a smart servant exists."

Both Slidells forced a laugh.

———————

As Robert emerged onto the windy terrace carrying the camera and tripod, Sylvia ran to him and gave him a kiss, then danced away. "Watch me! I'm queen of the forest." She twirled in the golden light of the setting sun. Two hundred feet below and on three sides, an ocean of oak trees, their leaves russet and scarlet and saffron, spread out to the horizon.

The stone mansion, livable, but not yet complete, sat on a karst precipice overlooking the 5,000 acres of Ozark forest Robert had bought two years ago. "Folly," people said behind his back. "Bully!" Robert rejoined, parroting his favorite politician. "It will be my private retreat, my castle."

Robert pointed the camera at Sylvia and started filming.

Kenyon, sleek and athletic, tried again to put an arm around Sylvia, but she pushed him away and dragged poor Howard, short and soft and deferential, to her side. "I like Howard best. You'll be my frog prince, won't you, Howard?" Then she pushed him away and twirled in the wind, her silk scarf a slash of crimson against a brilliant blue sky.

"Stand still!" Robert boomed at Sylvia.

Kenyon laughed. "No need to stand still, that camera makes moving pictures."

Robert glared at his son, instantly irritated at being corrected by his own son. He stepped up on the low stone wall that rimmed the terrace, and motioned Sylvia to do so too.

"Careful!" Kenyon cautioned her. "It's two hundred and fifty feet straight down."

"Better view up here, but trade places with me," Robert told Sylvia. "Get the sun on your face. You, Kenyon, stay out of the picture. This is about Sylvia."

Kenyon stepped aside, masking his hatred of his father.

The light was fading, but Robert kept the movie camera aimed at Sylvia smiling coquettishly. She backed away a step as Robert advanced.

A loose stone in the parapet grated and Sylvia was gone.

"She fell," Howard whimpered.

"I can see that, you idiot!" Robert bellowed. "Kenyon! Get the servants! Get down there and find her!"

It took them an hour to find her mangled body in the dark woods that lined the creek below the mansion. She was still clutching her red silk scarf. At the mansion they laid her body on a wooden table in the wine cellar and spread an ornate linen sheet over her motionless form.

While his father sat in his leather armchair scowling at the blazing fireplace in the mansion's central hall, and Howard sat sniveling and twisting his fingers, Kenyon marshaled the servants in the kitchen and told them Sylvia had fallen to her death. The women cried; the men removed their caps and shuffled their feet. Kenyon dispatched a groom to the village of Camdenton to fetch the sheriff.

Two hours later Oliger, the fat sheriff of Camden County, and his deputy, a lanky farm boy, stood in the wine cellar while Kenyon lifted the sheet over Sylvia's body.

They went out into the night wind on the terrace where by flickering lantern the sheriff examined the space where the stone had fallen from the parapet.

He craned over the edge at the blackness below for a moment, then the three men came in to stand in front of the fireplace.

As Oliger opened his mouth to speak, Howard lurched to his feet and sobbed, "She's dead…she's dead…" Fast as a striking snake, Kenyon grabbed Howard and hauled him up the curving stair like a sack of potatoes as Oliger and his assistant gaped at the spectacle.

In Howard's bedroom, out of hearing of the men in the great room below, Kenyon pulled Howard's face close to his own and snarled, "Shut up, you blubbering fool!" He slapped Howard once—hard, and threw him down in an armchair.

"I'm going to confess," Howard sobbed to Kenyon. "I killed her…"

Kenyon slapped him twice more. "No you didn't. She fell. Now shut up!" After a few more minutes of whimpering, Howard slumped into his armchair, and Kenyon made his way back downstairs.

Oliger closed the worn notebook where he had laboriously been making notes. "I'll make our my report tomorrow and…"

"You'll make out your report tonight," Robert interrupted. "At first light I'll be taking the body back to Kansas City for burial, and I'll need a copy of that report for the Jackson County sheriff."

"Yes, sir," Oliger replied meekly. He and his deputy settled their hats on their heads and departed.

Just before dawn, while Robert Snyder was supervising the loading of Sylvia's remains into a carriage draped in black crepe, Kenyon went to Howard's room and shook his brother awake. Several empty wine bottles sat on the table near the bed.

"I am going to accompany Father to Kansas City," Kenyon hissed at the bleary-eyed Howard. "You'll stay here and say nothing to anyone. You killed Sylvia, but I'm the only one who knows that, so you'll do exactly as I say unless you want to be hung for murder. I'll tell you when it's safe for you to return to Kansas City."

In Kansas City, Robert's influence got the inquest done, a modest burial plot purchased, and a quiet funeral arranged that same afternoon.

And so Sylvia McMath, Irish immigrant, age twenty, no known relatives, disappeared from the world.

Robert's wife Agnes maintained her regular social calendar with her friends. No one said a word, but the women's nods over tea or around the bridge table implied that it was God's will. They did not say mention the incident directly, but smug looks, knowing looks, implied Divine Retribution, a death well deserved.

Agnes maintained an icy silence, but inside she was seething. Not that her husband had a mistress, many successful Kansas City businessmen did, but he had allowed her existence to become public.

"It's a public scandal!" Agnes screamed at Nellie, her maid. "I wish Robert had fallen off that terrace! Not that…that… little fortune-hunting hussy!"

Robert moved out of the big family house on Rockhill road and into an apartment suite on Quality Hill. The stench of the Kansas City stockyards was strong here. But that suited Robert fine. He had made his fortune from those cattle, and their stench was the smell of money to him.

But things were not the same. His colleagues' attitudes toward him were different since Sylvia's death, and he became more and more reclusive.

Kenyon became the public face of Snyder & Sons.

———————

A month after the accident that took Sylvia's life, Kenyon sat in his office overlooking the Bottoms puffing an expensive Havana cigar.

That fool Howard did as I told him, loosened a stone in the parapet, But Sylvia fell, not Father. How was I to know they would trade places. If Father had died I would now have the company to myself.

He raised his eyebrows, tapped the ash from his cigar into the large glass ashtray on his desk. How easy it had been to convince pathetic Howard that Sylvia was in love with him and that getting rid of the father they both despised was the solution.

Kenyon jammed his cigar butt into the ashtray. *I need full control of this company. We can't go on having both Father and me trying to be president.*

After a while he gathered his hat and coat and had his private carriage take him to the Climax bar, one of the row of saloons that catered to the stockyard and slaughterhouse workers in the Bottoms. Every Tuesday and Thursday night, in a back room of the Climax bar, big Jim Pendergast held court. Big Jim was First Ward Councilman, the dispenser of patronage to the businesses connected with the stockyards, and the patron of the vast army of illiterate immigrant voters who worked there.

Kenyon had come to ask Big Jim for a favor, and he got it. Within a week Robert Snyder was dead, hit by an automobile on Paseo Avenue on a foggy night. The police never identified the car or the driver.

When the mail was delivered to the mansion, James,

the Butler, noticed Robert Snyder's obituary in the Kansas City Star and dispatched the upstairs maids to find Howard. Howard was eventually located in the dim wine cellar, opening his third bottle of wine for the day.

"Welcome," he slurred to James. "What news on the Rialto?"

The Butler masked his distaste for the dissipated young man and extended the newspaper folded back to the obituary page. "I'm sorry, sir. Grievous news."

"Read it to me," Howard told him.

The Butler stiffened in anger at being ordered by Howard. Howard remained oblivious to James' coolness. "Your father is dead, sir," James said, laying the newspaper on the wine-stained tabletop.

"There is also a telegram from your brother." James laid the telegram beside the newspaper and withdrew.

Howard's eyes slid across the newspaper column.

Prominent Kansas City Businessman Hit by Automobile

He topped off his glass and raised it. "*Vale*. Though I'm glad you're gone." He staggered to the wine racks, collected a bottle, and poured himself a full glass. "*Vita Brevis*."

After a period of basking in the glow of his father's demise, Howard thought to open the telegram from Kenyon.

Remain at the mansion. Kenyon.

Howard laid the telegram aside with a drunken smile. *That's no hardship. Out here I'm free of you and free of Father. Why should I leave this paradise?*

Candle smoke wavered in the minute whispers of air that infiltrated the wine cellar from cracks in the rock. Outside, the November wind was rising and snow flurries were breaking against the stone prow of the mansion.

———

Once in control of Snyder and Son, Kenyon ran the company with audacity and panache. And he quickly ran it into the ground.

In a year he took it from $1 million net worth to a negative $100,000. He lived well and ignored his creditors. Over cigars at the Kansas City Country Club, when Kenyon was out of earshot, his colleagues would remark that Kenyon seemed a man obsessed. Obsessed, not by making a fortune as his father had been, but obsessed with being always in motion, whether work or play. Always taking risks and demonstrating that he was fearless.

Some of his risky ventures paid handsomely, most did not.

Finally, his credit exhausted, he resolved to sell the one remaining asset he still held: the five thousand acres on which the half-built Snyder mansion stood. Lady Luck was smiling when he learned through a business connection in St. Louis that a syndicate of investors was intending to dam the Osage River. The dam would house turbines to generate electricity. Federal tax dollars would pour into the Ozarks to build the dam. The syndicate's lobbyists lavishly supported congressmen who supported the project.

Kenyon journeyed to St. Louis and during a lengthy conversation with the men of the syndicate, proposed that he deed his 5,000 acres to the syndicate. "This will demonstrate Camden County's support for the project." Kenyon told them with a beneficent smile. They agreed.

Kenyon's offer was accepted and in return he was appointed a non-voting member of the Osage Power Cooperative's board of directors. The position included a lifetime sinecure sufficient for him to live the lifestyle he enjoyed.

They all shook hands; cigars were lit. The Syndicate's secretary, a sharp faced, dour individual, said, "There is one small detail…"

Kenyon felt a knot of anger tighten in his stomach. "Yes, the mansion must be vacated. I realize that."

"By the end of this month," the man said briskly. He puffed his cigar and let the mellow smoke drift ceiling-ward. "Can you assure us of that?"

Kenyon nodded. "The house will be empty two weeks from today. I'll see to it myself."

———————

It was a long, dusty trip to the mansion, and Kenyon's flask of bourbon was empty long before he arrived. He stepped down from the rented carriage in a foul mood, slapping dust from his coat. "Find a place to sleep in the village," he snapped at the driver. "I'll need you to drive me back to the train station in Centralia tomorrow morning." Kenyon marched into the dank mansion and poured himself a brandy.

No servant came to take his coat and hat. Gloom and silence reigned.

"Howard!" Kenyon bellowed. "Where are you?"

The long walnut dining table was littered with dirty plates and serving dishes. A mouse skittered off the table and disappeared into darkness.

"Disgusting," Kenyon muttered.

"Howard?" Kenyon called into silence. He lit a candle, went upstairs, and searched the five bedrooms on the second floor. He found bedclothes in disarray, dirty dishware, cups and glasses, but no servants and no Howard.

Downstairs in the library the dust was thick. What could have been a bat flitted away from the top of a bookcase.

"Damned ruin," Kenyon muttered. He retreated to the main hall. "I should have come down here long ago and ejected that halfwit." He went down the stone steps to the wine cellar where he found dozens of empty wine bottles in a pile along one wall.

"Worthless drunk," Kenyon growled. His gaze fell on the wooden table where Sylvia's broken body had lain. His candle flickered in a cool breath of air. Kenyon, suddenly apprehensive, glanced around the room and cupped the candle to protect the flame. Then he chuckled. "No ghosts here."

———

In the main hall, Kenyon poured himself a second brandy. There was a faint noise from behind the closed reading room door at the end of the corridor. And a slit of light glowed under the door.

"Howard!" Kenyon bellowed. There was no answer so Kenyon stomped down the corridor to the door but found it locked. "Open up!" Kenyon pounded on the door. From inside room came a staccato clicking, a sound like a sewing machine.

Kenyon banged on the door. "I don't have time to waste…"

The door opened. Howard wavered there, drunk, a wine bottle in his hand. Behind Howard, Sylvia smiled at Kenyon!

Kenyon gaped at the flickering black and white image projected on the wall. The great projector clacked steadily as the film ran past the hissing white light.

"The film from Father's camera," Howard slurred over the racket. "I had it made into a movie." Kenyon stared at the wall where Sylvia smiled and twirled in an autumn breeze. She backed away a step, and then she was gone. The image disappeared for a few seconds then Sylvia returned, whirling her scarf in the autumn wind.

Kenyon grabbed Howard and slammed him back against the wall. "You perverted little bastard! I should throw you and that machine over the parapet."

Howard sagged against the wall, clutching his wine bottle.

The film went dark for a second then began again. Kenyon pulled Howard to his feet, but Howard twisted away. "No!" Howard shouted. "I love her. I have her now and always will!" His face was a ghastly white in the glare from the projector.

Kenyon, his eyes narrowed as they fixed on Howard, darted around the clacking machine. He grasped Howard by the neck, pushing him backwards against the wall. Howard, in a sudden fury, smashed his wine bottle down onto his brother's forehead. The glass shattered and Kenyon fell, blood spurting from a deep gash on his forehead. He clawed at his brother ineffectively as his vision dimmed. Howard staggered back and screamed with pain as his flailing hand met with the clacking steel teeth of the projector and was caught tight in the gears. The film slowed, then stopped. For an instant, a smiling Sylvia looked guilelessly down at the brothers. Then Sylvia's eyes turned to black holes, her beautiful face sagged into a nightmarish mask and disappeared in flame as the film burned through. Red-tinged black smoke poured into the room. Howard tried to pull free but succeeded only in pulling the machine over, pinning him under the hissing carbon rods. Howard's scream was lost in the roar of flame as the dusty carpet caught fire. In an instant the fire had spread to the heavy draperies, then the wood paneling.

In a few moments the entire mansion was ablaze.

As the residents of Camdenton gaped, the mountaintop inferno burned away the last traces of the Snyder brothers, cleansing them forever of greed and envy and lust.

Hart Land

Two brothers take very different paths in life as they attempt to achieve what they love most. But neither path is an easy one, and in the end, they find it even more difficult to assure themselves they have satisfied their love.

Even cloistered in the routine of farm life in early 1950s, the Hart brothers' personalities were beginning to show significant differences by the time James turned seven and Sam was six. James, thin and dark haired, with intense brown eyes, was more outgoing, more expressive, and more needy of his parent's time and attention, which was in very short supply. Sam, sandy-haired and a little chubby, was content to play by himself or follow James around. Sam especially liked it when James would lead the way to the little creek than ran through the farm.

The farm was all the boys knew, and farming was all their parents knew. Their father Walter Hart had come home from the army in 1946, married his high school sweetheart Adele, and bought four hundred acres of good Cooper county cropland.

Both Walter and Adele had grown up in Cooper county, and they loved the land, loved farming, and loved each other, though the boys never heard them say any of these things. The post-war economy was booming, the cold war did not touch the heartland, and commodity prices rose steadily year after year. Walter prudently bought more acreage with his profits.

Aside from Christmas morning, the boys got almost no attention from their parents. In fact, the Hart family only spent time together at meals. The boys accepted this as normal.

On winter days, when the radio said the roads were too icy for the school bus, Walter would drive the boys the five miles to school in Arcadia on the tractor. The boys enjoyed this. The warmth in the closed cab of the tractor with its diesel and cut-hay scents was cozy, and the presence of their father was a rare treat. "Got to work cattle, regardless of weather," he told them as the tractor rumbled down the icy road. "Work don't stop just because of a little snow and ice."

The nearest neighbors were two miles down Route J, which was still a gravel road, too far to walk, so except for at school, the boys never saw other children. Sam sometimes overheard James tell his mother he wanted to go play with other kids, but Sam never did.

Summer evenings, after chores and dinner, the boys would tromp along the fencerow to the little creek and explore. Seen close-up, there was endless variety, colors, textures, stones and twigs, leaves and dirt, bugs and frogs. They could not have articulated the feeling of their experience even if they'd felt like trying, but they were seeing the land, truly seeing it. And that sense of the land settled deep inside each of them. Some summer evenings they'd float inner tubes out on the little pond, diving down to the silty mud where the water was cold, and resurface to the humid summer air.

Things changed when James turned sixteen and stopped wanting to take Sam to the creek—or anyplace else for that matter. James wanted his own car. And for several tense months after his birthday, he spent every evening either arguing with his father about a car, or on the phone with his buddies. Eventually his father, worn out, consented. "You can have a car, but you'll have to buy it with your own money." Hay season would soon start, and James worked out a deal with his father to earn the car money he needed. His father would pay James fifty cents a bale for hauling and stacking the fifty-pound square bales.

Now that James was older and too exhausted after baling hay to go to the creek, Sam occasionally wandered down to the creek alone. Sometimes on a sunny afternoon he'd take his inner tube down to the pond and float around until the mosquitoes came out, but he got lonely going by himself. He tried to keep his imaginary games going, but it was different knowing James was not nearby. Because he became lonely, he was happy to go back inside the house where his father was collapsed in his chair in front of the TV, his mother doing dishes. No one ever said anything in the evenings. Too tired.

After some sharp words from his father about which of the two channels the living room TV would stay on, Sam convinced his mother to let him use part of his savings to buy his own television. They drove to the small Sears in Arcadia and returned with a GE black and white TV and set it up in his room.

After dinner and evening chores, Sam would go upstairs to his room and watch the TV shows he liked. Three days after Sam had bought the TV and was starting up the stairs to his room, his father lowered the

Arcadia News and gave Sam a meaningful glance. "If I find you're not keeping up with your homework because you're watching some crap TV show like *Twilight Zone*, I'm going to take that TV away from you." Walter raised his newspaper and continued reading while *The Red Skelton Show* played on the big Motorola in the living room.

By the end of August, over a thousand bales later, James had five hundred dollars and was ready to go car shopping. His father drove him to each of the two used car lots in Arcadia, and soon James' used Pontiac LeMans took its place in the gravel lot beside his mother's Oldsmobile and his father's Ford pickup. Now, every evening after wolfing down his supper, James would announce that he was going out driving around, and bang out the screen door.

When Sam turned sixteen, the car buying ritual was repeated: opening arguments, extra summer work to make enough money, then visits to the used car lots with his father. For Sam's car purchase, this involved visiting both used car lots in Arcadia on one Sunday afternoon, and all four lots in Grover the next. They looked at every used car that was for sale. Sam knew to let his father do the talking. Sam also knew that despite his father's grumbling about taking time to go look for a car when he should be out in the fields working, he liked bargaining for equipment. Walter took a lot of pride in his bargaining skills—pointing out each car's defects to the sweating salesmen, and working the price down to what he called a 'reasonable price' for his son's car.

Driving the stylish old Chevy home on Route J, Sam felt an elation he had not experienced since he had first explored the creek. For the next couple of months he was always manufacturing a reason he needed to drive in to the Shop-and-Go in Arcadia to get something. Coming home at dusk, down the familiar winding asphalt road, windows rolled down, and the clear air blowing in the scent of farmland, Sam felt a pure, serene happiness.

In his evening cruising through Arcadia, Sam soon noticed the Tastee Freeze on Route J was where the older kids congregated. He drove by the row of cars, the kids leaning on the cars sipping cokes and smoking cigarettes. He needed to be part of that. On the third evening driving by and scoping out the scene, he saw James' green Pontiac parked in the row of cars. James was lounging against the side, cigarette in his mouth. Sam was shocked and drove home. He avoided the Tastee Freeze for a couple of nights.

But three nights later, he cruised by and saw Mickey Thompson, a kid in his geography class, standing with the older teenagers. Sam parked and walked over to where James and two of his buddies leaned against the fenders of their cars. James flicked his cigarette away, "What are you doing here, Sam?"

"Nothing. Nothing," Sam said, trying not to show his nervousness. He waved at Mickey. "Hey Mickey, nice car." Mickey had the sharpest car in town, though everybody knew his father had bought the brand-new Pontiac he drove. "Yeah, thanks," Mickey said nonchalantly.

James continued joking with his friends, not really ignoring his brother, but not including him either. So, after a while, Sam took his ten-cent coke and went cruising around the other eight blocks of Arcadia.

The feel of Sam's old two door Chevy 210, three on the column, 235 cubic inch engine, was heaven. It was his, and it was freedom.

After high school, James and Sam in turn went off to Southern Illinois University, lived in the dorm, studied, and came back to the farm every school break, winter and summer, to work. Four years later they each emerged with a bachelor's degree in agricultural management, which had no effect whatsoever on their lives on the farm.

At college it had been easy to find girls you could ask out for a date. But back home, miles from town, finding girls to date, much less a steady girlfriend, was difficult. It was fifteen minutes just to get to Arcadia. And after Arcadia High School closed (followed quickly by the closing of the Tastee Freeze), it became a thirty-minute drive to the town of Grover, where there were people under sixty years of age. But Sam and James were up to the challenge and drove to Grover and back four or five evenings a week.

The boys did all the farm work now; Walter just supervised from the cab of his truck. Sam had gone from dreamy-eyed kid, to hard-working farm helper, to overweight high school nerd, to serious student at SIU, and back to hard-working farmhand. On the farm after college, Sam's fat melted away, and running the big equipment gave him confidence.

James took it for granted that Sam would do as he directed, just like he always had. In that respect neither of the boys had changed much, although they were now twenty-five and twenty-six. Sam was big and sandy-haired, stocky and muscular. James was an inch taller, wiry, reserved, hardheaded, and sported the same slicked-back 1961 hairstyle and dour expression he'd had since high school.

James hated working on equipment and would run a tractor two-hundred hours between oil changes, while Sam cleaned, serviced, and cared for the pieces of equipment like they were his children. Sam had developed his love of machines when dateless in high school. He'd spend his evenings and weekends tinkering with the engine in his aged 1955 Chevy.

James never joked, seldom smiled, and always needed a couple of days to make any decision. Sam on the other hand, had a ready smile, and could make a decision on the spot.

Walter just drove around in his big black Ford F350 looking at the calves, or the fields as the soybean crop was being harvested. But he still made all the major purchases. The implement dealer, the feed and pesticide dealers, and the people at the cattle sale barn all knew Walter's worth. All deals were handshake deals. Walter's banker would come around later and keep the paperwork straight on credit line and taxes. Walter never talked with the boys about how much money he had in the bank, but he would talk at length with the boys about his planting plan, or the purchase of a new combine to replace the old one.

———

After a short illness, Adele died of lung cancer in January 1986, only sixty-four years old. Walter took it very hard in his silent way.

When Adele had been alive, Walter, Adele, James and Sam would often have breakfast together before starting work. They never said much. But it was that coffee-scented family time that Walter missed the most after Adele was gone. Now he would sit alone drinking his coffee at the old kitchen table that Adele had bought at Furniture World in Arcadia forty years ago, back when Arcadia had had a furniture store, and a shoe store, and a small department store.

Walter never shared his feelings with James or Sam. But they both suspected that's what he thought about as he sat alone: the old days, when he and Adele had first started farming and the intoxicating feel of the land. Arcadia had been a real town back then.

But that was forty years ago. And now Arcadia was only an abandoned church, a few falling-down houses, and a checkerboard of empty lots, divided by the cracked asphalt that used to be Elm Street and First Street.

The summer after Adele died, Walter phoned both his boys and asked them to join him for coffee the next morning. At the table he told them, "I'm splitting this farm in half and giving each of you nine hundred acres.

Dave Jennings has got the paperwork. He'll be around to get your signatures next week."

The boys continued to farm Walter's eighteen hundred acres as though it was still a single farm. James and Sam would talk over all the big decisions, like what to plant in which field, when to harvest, and when to invest in new equipment. And Sam would usually defer to James, just as he always had.

At the breakfast table one morning in April, Sam announced he was getting married. "Met a girl in Grover, Cynthia Ashland. We've been going together a year now. She's great. You'll like her."

Everyone went back to their bacon and eggs.

"I suppose next thing you're going to tell me you're getting married…" Walter turned his gaze on James.

James finished his breakfast, took his plate to the sink, rinsed it, and put it in the dishwasher. "Going to re-stretch that loose wire in the fence on the west two hundred. Could use some help." The door banged shut behind him; Walter and Sam heard his boots clomp down the porch steps.

Sam got up and rinsed his plate. "I'll bring Cynthia by one evening this week." Then he went out to help his brother.

In time Walter and James met Cynthia, who had streaked blond hair, wore too-tight jeans that did not flatter her wide beam, and had a tendency to gossip after a couple of Bud Lights, though in part this was due to her nervousness about being around Sam's father and James, who tended to sit, saying nothing, unless she filled in the silences.

Sam and Cynthia's wedding was May 20th. James was best man, and everything went smoothly. When the couple returned from a packaged honeymoon in Hawaii, Walter told Sam he'd have a house built for him on the west two hundred acres.

A year later, as Sam and Cynthia were moving into their new home, James told his father he was getting married, too.

James wife, Agnes, was a girl he'd known since senior year at Arcadia High School. She had been a scrawny, plain looking girl then, and as the years passed, became a scrawny, plain looking farm wife, who said little, worked hard, and cared nothing about her looks or what she wore.

Walter had a house built for James and Agnes on the four hundred acres along Route J, the newest tract of land.

Life went on. The boys worked the eighteen hundred acres. Now that Walter and his sons no longer had breakfast together, Walter spent more and more time sitting on the couch staring at the land that had once meant so much to him. Cynthia and Agnes brought him food and cleaned his house on alternating weeks. Arcadia, which had had a population of twenty-five hundred when Walter moved to Cooper county in 1946, shrank to a convenience store/gas station. None of the farmers in the surrounding area cared much. The New Holland dealership, the John Deere dealership, the feed and seed supplier, the cattle sale barn, Foodland, and Rexall where they all shopped were in Grover anyway. But for Walter, there was now no reason to go into Arcadia, and Grover was too far to drive just to sit drinking coffee at McDonald's.

One day Cynthia told Sam, "It's really not right, leaving your father there by himself in that house. Arthritis in his hips—and in his hands so bad he can barely hold anything, and his blood pressure—who knows what all those pills the doctors have got him on are for? What if he falls down and breaks something, can't get up, can't call? He won't use a cell phone and won't use his hearing aids. I get by his house as often as I can, but..."

"I know," Sam told her.

"I'm not saying he ought to move in with us," she was quick to amend, "but he shouldn't live alone. He's got enough money in the bank, it won't be no hardship to... do something."

"I know,"" Sam told her.

"Well," she said to her husband. "Think about it."

"I will," Sam told her.

The subject was a tender one. Unlike his usual tendency to decide fast, Sam thought about it for a year and half.

It was lunchtime the first day of September, after all the hay had been put up that Sam finally came by to visit his father and talk about moving to assisted living. He found his father was still in bed.

"Can't hardly move my legs," Walter told Sam. "Don't feel no pain. Don't hardly feel nothing. Kind of numb-like."

Sam carried him to his truck and drove to the emergency room at the hospital in Grover. Then he got on his cell phone and called his wife, and then Agnes, who drove out into the fields and got James. They clustered together in the hospital waiting room not saying much.

"A small stroke, maybe more than one," the doctor told them a few hours later. "He should spend the night here."

"Can he walk?" Cynthia asked.

The doctor paused and their hearts fell. "After therapy, I would say your father may be able to get around using a walker, but for the near future he will need a wheelchair." The doctor turned to go. "You should be thinking about live-in help or an assisted living facility for him."

When Walter was released from the hospital, Sam and James and their wives drove him to Lakeview, an assisted living facility the other side of Grover. On the ride back to their homes, no one said anything. In the months that followed, each of them went by to see Walter often, sometimes twice a week, except during planting, or harvest, or calf, or hay season. And each time Walter seemed weaker and more withdrawn. He died a year to the day after he entered Lakeview.

———

Sam and James had begun working their acreages independently. With Walter gone, Sam had felt a need to do things his own way, to stop consulting with James over decisions he was perfectly able to make himself.

James didn't like this new arrangement much, and for the first time James felt some distance between he and his younger brother. Sam on the other hand, felt only a great sense of freedom. Something like the freedom he had felt the afternoon he had driven his first car home.

It was usually James whose farm looked best, even with all the contract help Sam used. Sam and Cynthia had gotten in the habit of taking a week's vacation every now and then, regardless of what needed to be done, or when. The bank had a travel club and arranged trips to Hawaii and Florida, and Sam and Cynthia took many of them.

James said nothing about this, but Sam knew it galled him. But it was Sam's decision to put up a turkey barn and do turkey raising for Tyson Enterprises that finally set James off. "That's not farming!" James shouted. "That's contract work. You're an employee."

"But that's where the money is, James," Sam said calmly, but like all things related to the land, logic did not rule. Sam went into contract turkey raising, and he and James stopped speaking to each other.

The years went by. The brothers saw each other less and less often. They'd still help each other during calving, hay, and harvest, but the jokes between them had ceased.

James and his wife lived a lifestyle so simple it could be called austere. They had no friends, and no activities outside of farm work. Sam's farm looked just as good, but it was dependent on contractors to plant, to spray, to cut and haul hay. By contract, Tyson paid him a check every ninety days when the birds were grown, but he still found himself dipping into the credit line more often than he liked.

One summer day Sam drove to the bank in Grover and used his credit line to buy a new combine. Two hundred thousand dollars of shiny green and yellow machine, but he wanted to have the first GPS-equipped one in the county, and John Deere had one for sale. "We can deliver on Thursday," the salesman said. Sam said he'd take it.

"Getting new equipment is the best investment you can make," Sam told Cynthia. "Less of my time doing maintenance, more time in the fields, making money." As always, he pushed worry out of his mind.

For ten years, Sam had found it was a lot easier to roll loans over than to pay them back. *After all,* he rationalized, *got to have new equipment or maintenance time will kill me. Got to have contractors, or I'll kill myself trying to get the work done by myself.*

Dave, his banker, said nothing when Sam added fifty thousand dollars to his annual equipment loan rollover and put the extra money in his checking account. The value of the land was much greater than his steadily increasing debt.

Sam and Cynthia seldom talked about much of anything any more, least of all Sam's brother and his wife. But once in a while, Sam and Cynthia would laugh about James' and Agnes' isolated, severe existence, hardly ever leaving the farm, not socializing at all. They paid for everything out of cash flow: new breeder cattle, the annual seed, feed and fertilizer, and maintenance on their old equipment.

"And when they die the only thing they will own is the farm," Sam said, felling both smug and forlorn at the same time. "Whoever inherits it, and it won't be us, will sell it to Con Agra. A lifetime of work and they won't get a cent of reward for it."

It was late August, the time of year when Midwestern farm work slows down for a couple of weeks. A good time of year. Summer was fading, and autumn hadn't arrived. Sam and Cynthia were just finishing lunch when the doorbell rang. Sam opened the door and was absolutely amazed to see his brother and Agnes standing there. The brothers had not paid a social call on each other for over fifteen years. Sam motioned James and Agnes inside. He was shocked to see his normally dour brother smiling. In fact, grinning from ear to ear.

Cynthia offered iced tea, but James said he'd rather have a beer; so cold cans of Bud were passed around.

"This is a real surprise," Sam told his brother. "You— taking time off in the middle of the day? What's up? Something wrong?"

"I sold the farm," James said.

There was no sound in the room for a full sixty seconds. "You sold some acreage?" Sam ventured.

"No, I sold the whole thing," James told him. "Sold the land, auctioned the equipment, livestock, house, furnishings, everything."

"Won't hardly need nothin' in Florida," Agnes said, her normal sour expression unchanged by the pending move. "Everything we own is wore out, no sense taking it with us. "

"We bought a lifetime residence subscription in a community called Clearwater Cove," James told Sam and Cynthia.

"I don't know what to say," Sam said finally.

"Alls you've got to say is goodbye and that you'll come visit. We've planned all this out. There's nothing left to do. And before you ask, I'll tell you why we decided to sell. It's because I'm seventy, too old to keep up with the farm, need more health care every year. You just can't operate a family farm when you're old. That's the fact of it. So my plan is to sell now, take the money, and make the rest of our lives secure."

A week later Sam watched their Dodge pickup pulling out of the driveway, bound for Florida.

The next winter, Sam and Cynthia did visit James and Agnes.

Every morning they'd go to breakfast in the clubhouse, sit at a round formica-topped table with other retired folk who ate in silence. Afterwards, the four of them would walk down the curving, perfectly manicured walkway back to James' and Agnes' condo. The Florida morning was already heavy with humidity.

"Over there's the assisted living apartments," Agnes pointed. "And behind that is the hospital."

Sam was glad to get back inside James' sterile apartment after the humidity outside. "When we bought here," James told him. "We bought the full plan. As our health needs increase, we move from section to section. And any time we need it, the hospital is always right there, with doctors and nurses on call twenty-four hours."

"Last stop in the plan is the full-care wing of the hospital," Agnes said quietly.

Sam, whose expression had been darkening said, "No, the last stop is the cemetery. I'm sure burial expenses were part of the plan you bought."

Agnes nodded.

"Sounds like your plan and their plan match pretty well." Sam's tone was surly. "They get all your money, and you get to live in this artificial...place. "

James frown deepened. "This 'place' takes care of us. No house maintenance, nothing. They bring clean towels and sheets twice a week."

"So what do you do all day long?" Cynthia ventured.

"Walk to meals and back," Sam snapped. "Or walk around in circles on the paths."

Cynthia tried to calm Sam, but his face was red.

James turned on him. "And what the hell are you doing all day? Driving around in circles planting and harvesting. Like we been doing for fifty years. You get to be seventy and you can't sit up in them tractor cabs ten hours a day any more. You got to stop sometime, and when you do, you need a plan for the rest of your life."

James turned on the TV and pretended to watch a golf tournament.

"This is all you got for four million dollars?" Anger

was high in Sam's voice.

James turned with the same look of condescension Sam had hated since they'd been kids. "You ain't learned nothin' yet, have you?" James sneered. "And you damned sure haven't saved any money." James laughed a dirty laugh. "I know how much you owe the bank, Sam. Smart people plan ahead, they don't go into debt, and you never was smart that way."

They sat looking at each other in anger.

Cynthia rose to take Sam outside, but James wasn't finished. "You remember Bill Pemberton, had a place out on Route M?" James continued. "He got old, wife was gone, had to sell the farm because he couldn't work it any more. Moved in with his cousin's family in Grover. Everybody hated it. Six months later they had power of attorney and stuck him in that shabby nursing home in Grayson. Skimmed off his money, too. Bill died, broke and alone. That's how you're going to end up, too."

Sam shook his head. No sense trying to tell his brother that this sterile existence wasn't life. It was some kind of candy colored air-conditioned waiting room at the funeral parlor.

Sam and Cynthia manufactured an excuse to return to Illinois and left that day.

"They don't do anything!" Sam's wife said, attempting

to calm Sam, who was still agitated. "Sit there and watch TV and talk about what the next meal is going to be. Watch TV after supper, then go to bed and get up the next day and do exactly the same thing. Nothing to see or do in Clearwater Cove, just endless empty curving streets, perfect little postage stamp lawns, nothing... They don't know a single soul in the whole place."

Driving up through the hills of Kentucky, Cynthia was restless and Sam was silent. She wanted to ask him how much they did owe the bank, but she knew that would just set him off again, and he would go through what a mistake it had been to buy the little house in Grover.

She knew it had hurt his feelings when she'd convinced him to buy a small house in Grover. "Just so I can spent a night or two there sometimes, be closer to my friends, that's all." She hugged him to reassure him. "I miss seeing my friends, and it's a thirty-minute drive each way just to get to Kountry Kitchen to meet Alice or Debbie for coffee." Neither one of them wanted to talk about the fact that they had been sleeping in separate bedrooms for two years.

The first summer after they bought the second house, Cynthia only spent a day or two in Grover every week or ten days. But now, a year later, she lived in Grover full time, spending only the occasional weekend with Sam at the farm.

Neither of them had confided in each other that they liked having their own space most of the time.

Four years after James and Agnes had moved to Florida, Sam went alone to Clearwater to visit his brother.

James was now in the assisted living section, and when the attendant rolled James out into the day room in a wheelchair, Sam did not even recognize him for a moment. James was seventy-two, but looked eighty-five. A withered, pale imitation of the farm boy Sam had alternately idolized and hated, sixty years ago.

Sam, still in a state of shock at his brother's decrepit condition, struggled to make conversation with James, but all he got was one-word responses. Shocked and hurt, Sam left, not even taking time to see Agnes, who was in a different wing of the building.

Back home, Sam sat alone on the living room couch one predawn spring morning sipping coffee. He liked that hour of the day best. He had been waking before dawn his entire adult life, and he liked it that way. The house was silent and held a comforting darkness all around him until the first pale greys and reds colored the eastern sky.

Sam was an intelligent man, though he never thought about the future or the past. But this morning was different. He was thinking about when he and his brother had been kids, the first day of summer, piling off the school bus, then down to the little creek to play an endlessly evolving adventure in which they were the last members of an ancient tribe, living on the prairie long before the white men came.

But those days were nearly sixty years in the past.

Yesterday, without telling Cynthia, he had driven to Grover and turned the farm over to the mortgage company to sell. "I'll just keep the house and the two acres it sits on."

Dave, his mortgage officer, had shaken his hand, "Well, Sam, I'm glad you came in. We've been getting a little nervous—all that debt. This bank's been bought out by a bank in St. Louis. They're focused on the bottom line, and farmland secured debt is not really the high performing consumer loans they're looking for. I've been putting off calling you. Well, it's done. Now we can both rest easy." Sam forced a smile.

Except that I still need money, Sam thought as he got in his truck. *Work at some mindless minimum wage job?*

At the house, Sam rinsed out his coffee cup, pulled on his jacket, and went out of the house and walked east along the fencerow, his mind ticking over the hundreds of times he'd driven a tractor across this land, massaging this ground until he knew every contour of it. He knew it better than he knew anything else in his life.

It took him ten minutes to reach the little creek not far from where his father's house had stood before he'd had the ruin bulldozed down. But the old elm tree was still there. He remembered when he and James had been kids, their father a tied a length of hemp rope to a limb, and the two boys had spent many an hour swinging from that rope, playing Tarzan, jumping out to land in the fresh cut bluegrass, rolling in the fragrant scent, finding four-leaf clovers.

The rising sun was a gold coin on the horizon. Sam reached the box culvert under the road, ducked through it and followed the little creek another hundred feet. The culvert and this little creek had been his and James' secret world. There were pools of water here and there among the rocks, now shiny blue and gold in the dawn light. He thought about the many hours spent exploring his little creek, lost in the vast flat fields. Sam saw with perfect clarity the color of every frog, every grasshopper, every rock and stick, and the bark on the willow trees along the creek, still wreathed in mystery and fascination, just as it had been when he was a kid. The lichens on rocks were grey, the moss a deep green despite the early spring cold. The chips of rock in the creek's little sinkhole were a double handful of white pebbles and flakes, marbled with iron oxide. He picked up one rock chip, and thought back to the arrowhead he'd found once. In all his visits after that, he had never found another.

As Sam sat along the bank of the little creek, he listened to the faint sounds of the creek and the fields. Sam put his face close to the dirt and breathed in the cool scent of early April. *This is where I belong: Close to the land.*

Radio Caroline

Kevin's life in London had become a nightmare of secrecy, fear, and paranoia. When an imagined threat turns real, only the lover he is afraid to trust may be able to save him.

Kevin woke in his darkened bedroom, hearing someone speaking softly in the next room. Cleo was not in bed beside him. His clock said 4 AM.

"Cleo?"

A voice, just at the limits of audibility went silent, and a moment later Cleo returned to the futon and slid under the sheets.

"What were you doing?" Kevin asked.

She lay still. "The radio was on," she lied. "I turned it off."

With an effort, Kevin suppressed his anger. "You are exceedingly difficult to trust, you know."

She turned away from him and was silent.

He slid out from under the covers and padded out to his office. At his desk, he checked the Nakamishi sound system. It was off. He opened what looked like a desk drawer and studied the security sensor screens there. Everything normal. No one but him and Cleo in his office and bedroom on this floor, and no one in his employee's offices on the floor below. He dialed back through the last four hours, but nothing was amiss.

Not satisfied, he got a hand torch and walked slowly through the office, then the bedroom scanning the top ledges over windows and doors, under cabinets and chairs.

After a time he returned to bed, tossed and turned.

"I'm sorry you feel that way," Cleo said into the darkness. "I've…my feelings have become rather strong for you, Kevin. It's more than nostalgia we felt for those days twenty years ago. I think you are a good person, driving yourself far too hard, and struggling with guilt that will only increase further with time."

His mind flashed with anger. "I don't really care to be analyzed at four in the morning," he told her, then rolled over, massaged his neck. "No, I didn't mean to say that, I'm sorry." He touched her back. "Since you've come to work with me here at HCA, I feel better. Things are better. You've done a superb job. And…getting to know you again after all these years has been wonderful. I hadn't realized how isolated I'd become."

They embraced. "I'm glad you feel that way. I do as well," she said.

"Why the frown?"

She pulled away from him and lay on her back, the sheets pulled up under her chin.

"The paranoia you feel, the fear. I've been telling you it's intrinsic to this kind of work. But there are…forces at work that will put you in danger."

He leaned on one elbow listening.

She told him about how she had been approached by a man, ordinary looking, completely lucid, who claimed to be from the future. And how she had come to believe him. His predictions of things were just too detailed, too accurate, to be chance.

"He told me two years ago that you would come into danger. This design, the explosive spider munition, is the reason. To protect you, I started working here. But to truly protect you I have to sabotage your bid for this contract with the Weapons Ministry."

"What are you saying?"

"There are competing forces among time travelers— no surprise, given human nature. At this time and place, your weapon system, the little explosive spiders, is a key factor in how the future will evolve. If the Ministry buys it, terrorists will quickly gain access to it, and certain national economies will be destabilized. But if the Ministry buys one of your competitor's weapons, all that will not happen."

"You believe this?" Kevin said. She could see his skeptical expression in the predawn light behind the window sheers.

"Yes."

Kevin rolled onto his side and pretended to sleep. As dawn light changed from grey to gold, Cleo left quietly. "I'll meet you at the Weapons Ministry."

At six Kevin showered, dressed in a dark blue bespoke suit he was fond of, with a white shirt and red tie. "Politicians colors," he snorted, but he knew it was necessary to make a conservatively good impression. He sipped espresso at the tall glass window of his office. Three floors below, raindrops glittered on black and red cars parked on Brewer Street. A nameless dread sat at the back of his mind like a tumor. He pushed the familiar paranoia away. "I need this contract," he told himself. "A million pounds sterling of post-prototyping alone, then the production oversight fees, testing...." He heaved a sigh and set his cup down on the corner of his bare Lucite desk. "Cleo," he muttered. "Time travel." He shook his head and called for the limo to take him to the Ministry. *I thought I was happy again, with Cleo, but if she's…* he let the thought evaporate. "What I really want," he told his reflection in the window, "is out. Out of this whole business."

———

The HCA team met him at an unmarked door in a nondescript warehouse near Canary Wharf. Weapons Acquisition Division preferred anonymity. Cleo looked sharp and professional in a very becoming purple Prada knock-off. The two HCA techs retained their post-doc dishevelment.

"Everything's ready," Cleo told him. Her confident smile betrayed nothing of the their earlier conversation.

They filed through multiple security checks, then upstairs to a small conference room overlooking an urban combat training mock-up, a block of empty buildings, bullet scarred from previous exercises. The buildings were wired for video and sound throughout.

This demonstration was a simple one for Brigadier General Breithwaite and his staff, so he could effectively answer questions at the press conference scheduled for later in the day.

The mechanical spiders were released into the buildings, and within seconds they were invisible, hiding in corners and cracks. An HCA technician zoomed a video in on the top of a door frame. "There," he adjusted the image to false color. "See it?"

The military men peered at the screen. "Just barely."

"They are virtually invisible to a casual search, and the explosive charge is below the limits of standard nitrate sniffers."

"Now, we'll activate their seekers," the HCA technician said. His fingers played over his keyboard and there was movement, flickers of movement at the edge of visibility as the cigarette sized spiders ran from hiding point to hiding point in a complex swarming pattern.

A row of green lights began to change to red as spider after spider located a target and placed itself within kill range. "This search mode software is the heart of the system," Kevin told General Breithwaite. "Complex swarming behavior with inter-unit communication. Very fast, very efficient, when compared to conventional pre programmed search patterns."

The row of twenty green indicators had all turned red. "Fifteen seconds," Kevin announced. "They've all found their targets. Cell phone repeaters, power transformers, the like: weak points in the enemy's power and communication infrastructure."

"Very impressive," Breithwaite puffed. He straightened his tie and glanced around at his minions. "What else should I know for the press conference?"

A canister lay on a table, open to display mock-ups of the munition. Silver cigarettes inside plastic tubes with black ends, the robots looked innocuous. Kevin picked one out of the canister and slid it out of its tube. Eight wire-thin legs sprang open.

"A barrage of these could bring a medium sized city's power and communications to a halt within an hour."

"How big a city?"

Kevin squinted. "Salzburg, Prague, Kiev, Manchester."

"Per unit cost?" one of the lieutenant colonels asked.

"HCA is offering these at one hundred forty thousand pounds for a canister of ten," Cleo told him.

"Fourteen thousand each," the other lieutenant colonel said noncommittally.

Breithwaite checked his watch pointedly, so Kevin concluded the demonstration with the effusive thanks expected from contractors.

The HCA employees piled into the two limos Kevin had hired for this purpose and were driven back to HCA's office on Brewer St. At the corner of Brewer and

Regent, Kevin told the driver to stop in front of the Brewer Street Arms pub.

"Too early for a celebratory drink?" Kevin queried.

"Never," Ian and Colin chorused.

They dashed through a misting rain and took up their usual places in the cracked but comfortable naugahyde chairs round a worn black table.

"Thought the demonstration went well today," Ian said. "But we need to start thinking about the next generation." Paul said. "Which is..."

"...Anti-personnel," Ian finished for him. They dove into an animated conversation, while a silent Kevin slumped in his chair staring at his glass of Jameson's whiskey.

"Easy to re-mission our little pet robots," Ian said.

"Moving targets, though, a bit more..."

"That's where the swarming-algorithm's strength is. Instantaneous corrections as the target moves."

"And," Colin added, "the current explosive is big enough to do the job if it's on the enemy soldier, not just near him."

Paul laughed sarcastically. "Delightful little beasts. Explosive is enough to remove a head or an arm. And each no bigger than this." He pulled a box of Players cigarettes from his pocket and extracted one.

"No smoking, sir," the waitress said.

"And troops can saturate an area in advance of enemy infiltration. They're virtually undetectable in urban terrain."

Cleo watched Kevin's frown deepening as the conversation proceeded. "Don't dwell on all this." Cleo said quietly.

The pub was getting noisy as the lunch crowd began to fill the tables.

Cleo's phone buzzed. She stepped away. Ian noticed her cast an ambiguous glance back at Kevin. After a moment more, she put her phone away and touched Kevin on the shoulder. "I need to run a quick errand. But I'll be back, promise."

He shrugged, picked up his glass, and drank half. He rolled his head, loosened his tie. "This is no way to live, believe me."

Cleo knelt and looked him in the eye. "Promise me you'll stay here. Have another drink. You deserve it. But stay right here; I won't be a minute." Cleo waved the bar maid over and signaled for another round. Then she collected her raincoat and was gone.

There was no one in the Aroma coffee shop when Cleo got there. Rain blowing down Regent Street tapped the windows. Cleo got an espresso and sat at a table by the window waiting anxiously. Steam misted the glass, making the hurrying pedestrians outside into an impressionist painting. A moment later Mike Dace arrived, wearing a blue Burberry. He wrestled the door closed, furled his wet umbrella, tossed it into the chrome bin, ordered a latte, and then sat down beside Cleo, keeping his coat buttoned.

"You need to move Kevin out of this timeline immediately," he said without preamble. "You heard the radio communication last night. You have completed your assignment. You've put the fatal flaw in the HCA budget proposal. The Ministry will award the contract to Tetratech, not HCA. Their prototype will not go into production."

His latte was brought to him. He removed his glasses and polished the steam off them. "Within twenty-four hours an attempt will be made on Kevin's life which will likely succeed, and if it does, the Ministry will reconsider their decision not to buy HCA's munition. He needs to be out of harm's way tonight. We've already planned how to explain his disappearance. Move him tonight."

"The detection systems in his flat and office are good," Cleo said. "Another day or two and I can convince him to take a long vacation, away from all this. Tetratech will have won the contract..."

"Tonight," Dace repeated.

Cleo sipped the bitter black espresso.

Dace placed his glasses back on his face. "Don't keep him here, risking this whole operation, just because you enjoy sleeping with him. I advised you not to get involved with him two years ago when you agreed to this assignment."

Cleo shook her head, near tears. "Don't talk any more. Just don't speak." She left her coffee and hurried through the rain to the pub.

Everyone was still there except Kevin.

"Gone where?" Cleo gasped, out of breath.

"Back to his office," Paul said, with a know-it-all-smile. "Likely needs your help."

At the HCA building it took her three tries with her wet security card to get the door open.

Upstairs, the office was dark; Kevin was standing near the big window overlooking Brewer Street.

"I hate this, all of this." He looked at her in the dim red light from the street signs below. "This is someone else's life. I didn't set out to do this."

Cleo stilled her breathing, caught his arm and led him to the sofa. "Remember 1966? That old house in Earl's Gate? Remember? We were happy then. That's where we first met, before you decided you had to go to San Francisco." Cleo said. She took his arms—led him to the sofa. The rain was soft on the tall glass windows.

"1966," Kevin mused. "You don't know how many times I've wished I was back there. But I am here twenty years later, praised and paid for thinking up newer and ever more efficient bits of death, in a red queen's race."

A car moved slowly past on Brewer street, momentarily putting a soft glow of light in the room.

Kevin held his finger to his lips.

He pulled the velvety microwave-absorbing sheers carefully closed. With the hand torch he kept always at hand, he walked through the darkened loft, eyes and ears straining for the slightest indication of the metallic insects he knew so well. He swept the light through dark corners, the top edges of door frames and windows. That's where they would be waiting, clinging flat, waiting for his heat signature to trigger them. At the control panel he checked the motion and heat sensors and ran a diagnostic, then clicked the cover closed. But he felt no more secure.

"A double agent could plant the little devices in this

room." He said. "Might even be you."

Her expression twisted in anguish. "This will be hard for you to understand. But I can save you."

She showed him her watch. It displayed the correct time, but there were other buttons. She explained time travel. His expression didn't change.

"This is difficult to believe, you know. What do these futurists look like?"

"Ordinary people." She said. "They've traveled back to our present."

"For what reason?"

"To affect changes."

"Why?" he asked.

Cleo shrugged.

"Why do you do it?"

"Money," she said flatly.

"What is the cause for which your side strives?"

"Probably unknowable by us."

"It seems so wrong, altering history without regard for consequences…"

She turned away from him.

He took a deep breath. "You sound a bit like fascists—never questioning the cause, holding a fervent belief in something just because it is powerful, and you've been told it's right. The Nazis used the same propaganda."

She said nothing for a moment, then turned back to face him in the dim light. "Is what you're doing so different? Selling your little robot bombs for money. How long will it be before extremist groups have them, a year perhaps?"

Kevin rolled his head. "My neck hurts—tension. Yes. I hate all this. Weapons, killing, I want out."

"But you can't get out. Your competitors, our government and others, extremists groups, common criminals—they all want the latest technology of death. Which exists in *your* head. Someone will have it, or someone else will kill you, so that their enemies won't get it."

"I am going to get out," Kevin said softly. "This business is literally driving me crazy. I'm afraid the robot munitions have been planted in this flat."

Cleo took him in her arms. "The futurists I work for want you out of this business too, but they won't kill you to do it. The time device is a foolproof escape. Let me send you back in time."

Kevin pulled back to look into Cleo's eyes. "What if I go back in time? Can I come forward again?"

"No," Cleo said. Her voice quivered. "It's one way. And you'll still be the age you are now," Cleo warned. "You'll be forty, older by far than your friends. Another you will also exist there. The younger you."

"Then send me back to the summer of 1966, London in the first full bloom of innocence that was the peace and love of the 1960s. The last time that I was truly happy."

Cleo nodded slowly. "That would work. By the time the other you returns to London the timelines will have diverged and you'll never confront each other precisely because you stayed in London and did not go to America."

He frowned, snorted, then grinned. "That's assuming this time device is real and that you're not just another crazy subject to delusions, like me. It must be quite empowering to be among the last of the Time Lords."

But Cleo didn't laugh at his joke; instead she responded with an allusion she knew he would get. "No, it feels more like being one of the Kyben, suspended by a medallion from the time mirror."

"Don't be sad." He embraced her.

"I'll never see you again," she said.

"This me is not so lovable. We would not do well together."

"But I do love you. Maybe we could…"

He shook his head. "You told me yourself someone will try to kill me. They might just succeed." He saw the silvery streaks of tears on her face as she adjusted the device on her wrist.

"To the Tardis, Doctor," he teased, but his joke fell flat.

She stepped into the doorway where the light was better. "When you find me back in 1966, it will be the younger me, not this me, not the me that loves you so much, and never wants to lose you." She finished her adjustments and looked up at him, her expression sad but fierce. "Find me and make sure we stay together. I loved you then; I just didn't realize it until later. Keep us together. Promise me."

"What will happen to you, this you?"

"I'll be fine. And one more thing. After you've traveled back in time, I can speak to you once, but only once. That capability is designed to assure you've arrived. Listen to Radio Caroline, 24.5 megahertz on the medium wave band."

Kevin nodded.

"Listen at midnight September 14th," she continued. "After you've heard the message, heard me speaking, phone the station and thank them. And that's the end of it."

She began to sob.

Out of the corner of his eye, he caught a glimpse of familiar movement, something on the top of the door frame.

"Cleo! There's a device on the door frame! Get clear!"

Cleo took a step toward him, there was a sound like scissors closing, and he heard her say, "I love you, Kevin." Then darkness engulfed him.

———

He was standing before a door. A much painted and repainted door to the front gate of a row of brick houses. He knew this place. Earl's Gate, London. He turned the knob, went in, walked down the brick path to the open door of the house and into a room hazed with smoke, full of people.

And there was Cleo. Cleo with her hair cut in Joni Mitchell bangs, sitting cross-legged on a faded paisley cushion puffing a joint, then laughing. He threaded his way to her: someone pressed a can of Double Diamond beer into his hand.

"Thought you were off to San Francisco," she said. How young she looked!

"I went. Now I'm back."

On the walls were concert posters, photos of Chairman Mao, and the Buddha, hand-painted psychedelic patterns in Day-Glo orange.

Joints circulated, Radio Caroline played.

He took her by the hand and they threaded their way through the dark kitchen, drawn by the sunshine scent of the garden.

At the back wall of the garden was a weathered bench surrounded by verbena. There was a thicket of fragrant mint at the brick wall. Bees buzzed nearby.

"That lot's taken to calling me Sandy," she said.

"Why's that?"

"Think I look a bit like Sandy Denny. Fairport Convention. Love their stuff."

"Don't follow her example," Kevin said. "Drugs and drinking. It will end badly."

She eyed him. "I want more than that," she said a bit defiantly. She studied his face. "It must have been a difficult trip. You've aged. You told me you might not be coming back at all."

"You haven't changed," he said with a smile. "And that's good. I was foolish to leave." He kissed her. "Where does the time go?"

She laughed at his allusion: an open, beautiful laugh. He remembered it well.

———————————

The days passed. It was as though he had never left. Kevin and Cleo watched the summer rain fall, smoked dope and drank cheap wine from the bottle. Read the classics old and new, in used paperback editions they bought in the bookstalls on Portobello Road.

And that was all he wanted for now, to just live this moment with Cleo. Lying in the sun in the garden, reading Blake, Burns, Coleridge, Byron, Shelley, Rimbaud. Or lying together on a futon in the stillness at three in the morning, candlelight flickering over the high ceiling and dusty wallpaper of the old house.

The world really was his, his and Cleo's, and heaven really was in a wildflower. Candlelight on filigreed wallpaper in the deep green of summer Chelsea gardens.

Down the hall, in the room where Peter and Angie slept, Peter kept Radio Caroline playing most nights. Much of the time they played American blues and other music of little interest to Kevin, but at midnight they played some of the best of the growing British rock scene.

It was September 14th, midnight, the time Cleo in the future had told him to listen for her message. Kevin slid out of the sheets and padded down the corridor to stand in the darkened hall where he could hear the radio clearly.

A song ended and, instead of the regular announcer, there was Cleo, whose voice he knew so well, sounding sad but resigned. "Hello Kevin. This is Cleo, your Cleo. I hope you are listening. In the past we both remember, we let our lives diverge. This time I hope you will keep us together. You have a chance to put things right for both of us. I miss you terribly, but I know that you are with the other me, and that the two of you can live the lives you and I wished for. I'll never see you again, and that hurts terribly, but this is what's best. They tried to kill you once. They would have tried again until they succeeded if you'd stayed here. Goodbye, Kevin. I love you."

There was silence for a moment, then the music resumed, the Rolling Stones' *Out of Time.*

Kevin glanced at the top of the hallway door-frame in the dark, his old paranoia returning for a moment. But in this universe, none of that had been invented yet.

And he need not invent it.

He found a phone downstairs, called the station, and thanked them for the dedication to Kevin. Then he went back upstairs.

The scrape of a match startled him. A candle's glow lit their bedroom at the end of the hall. "Are you there, Kevin?" Cleo said sleepily. "Where did you go?"

He slid under the sheets and kissed her. "Yes, I'm here." He blew out the candle. "I love you."

"I love you too, Kevin. I woke and you were gone."

"I won't be leaving again."